Zombie Park Crew
The Sports Dimension

Created by Melissa and Tysen S.
Illustrated by Katharina, Tysen, and Melissa

For: Miss Coleman
Mrs. Thompson
Mrs. Josephson
Mrs. Shaffer
Mrs. Gehler
Ms. Nelson
Mrs. Johnson
Mrs. Benson
Mrs. Monssen
Mrs. Schulz
Ms. Zirbes
Mrs. Bonde
And all the other great teachers out there

Chapters

Zombie Park (1)

"What would you rather be: a T-rex or a megalodon?" Ruby asks me, her blue eyes widening excitedly.

"Oooo, that's a good one!" I think about this. "I'd rather be a megalorex," I say.

Ruby looks puzzled. "What's a megalorex?"

"It's a creature with a tyrannosaurus's head and a megalodon's body, but it would also have legs so it could swim in the water or walk on land."

"First of all, that's cheating," says Ruby. "You have to choose one or the other, Sawyer. Secondly, that is terrifying! Although, if I were being chased by one, I'd just throw a puff of smoke behind me so he couldn't see where I was going and climb up a tree." Ruby is really good at chemistry stuff — and at climbing trees.

We grab our backpacks and get off the bus. It's the first day of third grade, and I'm excited. Two of my best friends, Ruby and Olivia, are in my class. Hudson is my third best friend. The three of us met before we were born. Yep, you heard that right, before we were born. Our moms took a baby class together when they were pregnant. I'm also excited because Mr. Watkins is our teacher. He's basically the coolest third-grade teacher at Hawkins Elementary.

Ruby and I wait on the sidewalk for Hudson and Olivia to get off the bus, and we all walk toward the entrance together. Well, actually Ruby doesn't walk. She skips, shouting, "Look out! Ruby's coming through," as she goes along.

We get to the hallway for the third-grade rooms and wave goodbye to Hudson. "See you at recess," I say. Olivia, Ruby, and I turn left to Mr. Watkin's room.

Mr. Watkins is standing outside the classroom, wearing a checkered bow tie and jeans. "Olivia! Ruby! Sawyer!" he yells, raising his hand so we can each give him a high five. "Find your desks and unpack your backpacks, then find your lockers and put your backpacks in them."

Olivia finds her desk immediately. "Yes! I'm in the front!" she exclaims. Oh, I should mention that Olivia really likes school. I mean, like REALLY likes school. Basically, school is her favorite activity. Teachers always really like her, too. She is always the first kid in the class to win the Student of the Month award. Always.

I find my desk at the back of the room. It's one of those desks where you open the top and there's room for all your stuff underneath. I open the top and start to unpack my backpack. I have the usual stuff: pencils, notebooks, erasers, comic books about aliens attacking our galaxy, sour candy, comic books about T-rexes attacking cavemen, a ruler, and folders. I look around to see where Ruby's desk is. Hers is by the door. She's talking excitedly to Darnell as she unzips her backpack, opens the desk, and dumps all the backpacks contents into the compartment.

"Did everyone get their stuff unpacked?" Mr. Watkins calls as he enters the room. "Be sure to also find your locker and hang up your backpack."

I walk to the side of the room and find the locker with my name on it. It also has Olivia's name on it. "Hey, we're locker buddies again," I tell her. "I call the hooks on the right!" I put my stuff on the hook.

Olivia doesn't share my enthusiasm. "I should just tell you right now, this year I'd like you to try not to be as messy," she says.

"I'm not *that* bad." I say this out loud, but in my head, I know she's right. My locker is usually the one where things fall out when you open it. But at least it's not as bad as my bedroom. Whoa, man! My bedroom floor is always so covered in stuff that you can't see what color the carpet is. On the positive side, though, it's really easy to play *the floor is hot lava* in my room.

Mr. Watkins shows us our daily schedule, which he's written on the whiteboard.

8:30-8:45 - Daily Math
8:45-8:50 - News
8:50-9 - Morning Meeting
9-10:15 - Reader's Workshop
10:15-10:30 - Number Corner
10:30-11:20 - Writer's Workshop
11:20-12:10 - Specialist Class
12:10-12:35 - Recess
12:35-1:05 - Lunch
1:05-2:05 - Math Workshop
2:05-2:30 - Word Study
2:30-2:40 - Planner
2:40-3:10 - Clean Up / Stack Chairs
3:10-3:45 - Dismissal

I raise my hand. Mr. Watkins nods at me, and I ask, "when do we have snack time?"

Mr. Watkins adjusts his bow tie. "In third grade, there isn't snack time."

Gasp! No snack time? I think about the crackers sitting in my backpack and the sour candy in my desk. My stomach rumbles. I look at the clock. It's only 8:37 and I'm already hungry. I look over at Olivia, who is listening attentively to Mr. Watkins. I look at Ruby, who also has a look of surprise on her face. Then she shrugs her shoulders, takes an eraser that looks like a small piece of pizza out of her desk, and pretends to bite it.

The first day of school is full of ups and downs. Our specialist class is Computer (up), recess mostly consists of listening to rules (down), lunch is pizza (up), and there's no time for me to read a comic book (down). It takes forever to get to 3:45. Like, *forever.* It feels like one day of third grade was as long as the entire second grade. Finally, we get to the bus. This time I sit next to Hudson.

"Dude, do you know what the worst part of third grade is?" he asks me.

"No snack time," I grumble.

"No snack time!" he repeats. "I was starving by lunchtime."

Olivia and Ruby are sitting in the seat across the aisle. Olivia looks at us. "Well, unhealthy snacks can lead to obesity, so I'm sure it's a good thing that they don't have snack time this year." She brightens. "Plus, now there's more time to learn!"

Ruby shakes her head at Olivia, then looks at me. "I vote we go home for a snack, and then meet at Zombie Park at 4:30. All in favor, say 'aye.'"

"Aye."

"Aye."

"Aye!"

I get home and drop my backpack on the ground. Mom is working in her office. She looks up from her work computer. Everyone says I look like her. We have the same round face, the same brown hair and green eyes, and the same smile. "How was school, Honey?" she asks.

"Argh, please don't call me 'honey'." I'm frustrated because I've told her this a hundred times. I'm eight now, way too old to be called something like that. "My name is Sawyer. School was good. I'm going to get a snack and then meet the crew at Zombie Park."

"Sounds good, Sawyer. There are apple slices in the fridge. I have a work call. Be home by six for dinner. Then I want to hear more about your day!" Mom goes back to her computer. To be honest, I'm not sure what her job is. Apparently, she gets a lot of emails and has a lot of calls over her computer. That's all I know about it.

I walk into the kitchen, open the fridge, and grab the apple slices. I get some peanut butter from the cupboard. *Mmmmm, apple slices and peanut butter!* I know some kids are allergic to peanuts, and I feel bad for those kids. Hmmm, maybe someday Olivia will invent a cure for kids who are allergic to peanuts. That would probably make her rich, and then she'll probably buy super expensive gifts for me. Like a car. Or a house. Or a space-ship. Or a house that can turn into a space-ship, and it also has wheels so it's also a car.

I finish my snack and run upstairs to grab my Zombie Park backpack. Each of the crew has one of these. We fill it with stuff we can do at the park. Mine has sour candy (of course) and comic books (of course) and bases that we can use for *the ground is hot lava*. I run down the stairs and grab my scooter. Olivia's house is on the way. When I get there, she's sitting on her front porch step, reading a book. "Hey," I yell with a wave. She waves back, grabs her Zombie Park backpack off the step and puts it on her back, then grabs her scooter and rides up to me.

"What were you reading?" I ask as we head off toward the park.

"The encyclopedia."

"The encyclopedia?"

"Yeah. Specifically, letter C. Did you know a caribou can weigh seven hundred pounds?"

"No. No, I did not know that," I say. I wonder if Olivia can hear the boredom in my tone.

"And even the female caribou has antlers. Did you know that?"

"No. No, I did not know that." I'm feeling more bored by the second.

"And it can run fifty miles an hour?"

"Hey, look," I say, quickly changing the subject as we enter the park, "Hudson and Ruby are already here."

We pass the Garden Park sign, which is sur-rounded by blooming flowers. I should mention that just the crew and I call this park Zombie Park. One day, we were lying in the grass and watching the fluffy clouds above us when Ruby said Garden Park sounds boring, so we should call it something else. We came up with all sorts of names and Olivia wrote them down. I was the one who suggested Zombie Park. Doesn't that sound cool? If I ever actually saw a zombie here, I'd just pull out the water gun that I keep in my backpack and squirt him in his face until he turned in the other direction. Zombies don't like water. I don't think I'll ever actually see one here, though. This is a safe neighborhood. Also, zombies aren't real.

Ruby and Hudson are playing fetch with Liz. Liz is Hudson's black lab. She runs up to greet Olivia and me. I balance the handle of my scooter against the "for sale" sign for a house next to the park.

"Lizard!" Olivia calls, petting the dog on the head. I pet her too. Hudson named her when he was four. He went through a phase where he was obsessed with lizards. But his parents thought a dog would be a better pet for a kid his age.

"Think fast!" Ruby yells and throws the tennis ball at me.

I do not think fast. It hits me in the face. "Ouch," I say. I rub my cheek. It hurts a little, but not too badly.

Ruby laughs. "Throw it back!"

I pick it up and throw it. It isn't a good throw, but Ruby runs and catches it.

"What did you guys have for snack?" Olivia asks, catching the ball when Ruby throws it to her. "I had grapes and crackers."

"Apple slices and peanut butter," I say.

"Carrots and ranch," says Hudson.

"Three slices of pizza and four cookies," says Ruby. I'm not surprised by this. Ruby eats a lot. "What else should we play?"

"I have the spy gear in my bag," offers Hudson. He walks to his Zombie Park backpack and pulls out four Spy Packs. Spy packs are these little bags that have all the gear spies use, like magnifying glasses, fingerprint powder and brushes, flashlights, even a pen that records what you say. Hudson pulls out a spy hat and sunglasses and puts them on. The rest of us do the same. "Hmm," he says, leading us toward the weeping willow tree. "Ah-ha! A clue!" He grabs his magnifying glass and looks closely at something on the ground.

I walk over and see that he's looking at a glove. It's one of those stretchy cotton ones, the kind you wear in cold weather. It's bright blue and has a picture of a wizard hat on it.

"Whoever lost this glove… he's the culprit!" Hudson says dramatically. He picks up the glove.

"Yeah," Olivia chimes in. "He's the one who stole Ms. Miller's pearl necklace!"

"There must be more clues nearby. Everyone search," I tell them. We all walk in different directions, keeping our eyes on the ground. As I'm looking near the twisty slide, I feel something hit my back. I look at the ground to see it was a pine cone. I look up to see if it fell off a tree branch. Then I get hit again with a pine cone. This one came from the direction of the rock climbing wall.

"Hey!" I hear Olivia cry. I look over to see a pine cone hit her, and another on the ground at her feet. Those, too, came from the direction of the rock climbing wall.

"Who's there?" Hudson calls. A pine cone comes soaring toward him and he catches it. Another flies toward Ruby and she catches it. She throws it back and we hear an "ow" from behind the rock climbing wall.

"Got ya!" Ruby calls. "Let's find out who it is!" She runs toward the wall, and the rest of us follow.

The pine cone thrower flees toward the woods that border the park.

"Red shirt, black pants, short brown hair, about four feet six inches," Olivia says as she watches him run away.

"Come on! Let's follow him!" Hudson grabs Liz's leash and we run into the woods. "Which way did he go?"

We all stop and look at each other. I shrug my shoulders. "We could each go in a different direction to see if we can find him."

"I'm not supposed to go farther than this," Olivia says.

"Me neither," Hudson adds.

Ruby stomps her foot. "Darn! We didn't see his face!"

Hudson slides his spy sunglasses up on his head and looks around the woods, his finger curled under his chin as if deep in thought. "Maybe he's the same culprit who the glove belongs to."

"Maybe the wizard hat on the glove is a clue," I add. "Maybe it's a magic glove."

We all look at each other, excitement on our faces as we imagine what a magic glove might do. I picture it making a sour candy appear out of thin air whenever I want one. An alarm chimes from Ruby's watch. "I gotta get home. I have soccer practice."

"I should go too," says Olivia. "I'm excited to read more about the caribou." She looks at Hudson and me. "Are you guys staying here?"

Hudson looks at me. "I'll stay if you will."

"I will, too. We'll see you guys tomorrow," I say, stretching my hand out to Ruby. I have a unique high-five with each of my friends. Ruby and I high-five, then high-ten. Then Olivia and I high-five, then do double fist bumps.

As they walk away, Hudson holds out the glove toward me. "You should put the glove on so we can test its magic."

"Okay," I say. I put the glove on my right hand. It makes my hand feel warm, which is normal for a glove to do. But then the warmth spreads. It feels like a heated blanket has been put on my arm. Then the heat spreads to my shoulders, to my face, and eventually to my entire body. It's soothing, but strange. "Whoa."

Hudson must have noticed the surprise on my face. "You okay?"

"I'm good," I say, but I take the glove off. Immediately, the warmth is gone and I feel normal again. "That was weird. You should try it on."

I hand it to Hudson, and he puts it on. "Whoa," he says, and I can tell he's feeling the same thing I did. "It feels like I'm standing in front of my fireplace."

"Do you think this really is a magic glove?"

"It's probably just some sort of new technology. Have you ever tried heat warmer packs for your hands? Something like that. Let's have the girls wear it tomorrow." Hudson takes the glove off and puts it in his backpack.

We play fetch with Liz for a while longer and talk about the magic glove. Then we say goodbye and I ride my scooter home. As I ride up my driveway, I see both cars are in the garage. That means Dad and Lana are home now. Lana is my little sister. She's two and she goes to daycare during the day. Dad always picks her up after work. She is loud and spoiled. She also really, really likes me. When I open the door, I hear her call my name. She runs to me for a hug and a kiss on the cheek.

Let me be clear. The only girls that I would let kiss me on the cheek are my mom, my grandmas, and my sister. I would never let another girl do that. Ew. Well, maybe I'll let another girl kiss me on the cheek when I get married. But I'm not getting married until I'm *at least* thirty. Why thirty?, you might wonder. Because that's when you're old. And when you're that old, you probably won't be alive much longer anyway so why not get married?

We have tacos for dinner. I'm super hungry so I eat three of them. Mom says the same thing she always says when I eat a lot: "You must be growing!" We talk about our days. Dad had a mean customer and Lana played with Play-Doh. Sometimes I wish I were two again so I could just play all day. I mean, sometimes school is fun, but there is just so much learning. Learn, learn, learn. All day. If I were a teacher, I wouldn't make my class learn *a thing.* They'd probably vote me Teacher of the Year.

We watch some TV after dinner, then it's bedtime. Mom makes me read to Lana at night. She says it's good for our brains and our bond. Do you know what that means? Me neither. I always try to read a comic book to her, but Lana insists on reading about princesses, baby animals, or unicorns. We brush our teeth, put on comfy clothes, and I play Legos quietly in my room until lights out. It's the same thing. Every. Single. Night. I wish Mom would shake it up some, you know? Like maybe one night, instead of reading, we could take a haunted house tour. Or, instead of brushing our teeth, we could just chew some mint-flavored gum. Or, instead of quietly playing Legos, I could practice playing the drums. I think *that* would be good for my brain.

That night I dream I'm back at Zombie Park with the crew. I have the magic glove. I put it on and feel the same warm feeling flood over my body. The crew and I are playing with Liz. I reach down to pick up a stick to throw for her.

"Ahem," I hear someone clear their throat. I look up and see a short, stout man in a pink wizard hat. He has a wrinkled face and a big nose.

"Who are you?" I ask.

The wizard ignores my question. "The glove," he says, nodding toward my hand.

I wonder if the glove belongs to the wizard. Should I offer it back to him?

As if reading my thoughts, the wizard continues, "It belongs to you and your best friends now."

"Okay, thanks. I know it will keep my hand extra warm this winter."

The wizard chuckles. "Oh, that's not all it will do."

I wonder what he means. I picture a glove that can magically turn into a calculator. Man, that would come in-handy during Math Workshop. "What else can it do?"

"Think about what other dimensions you'd like to visit. The glove can take you there."

I wake up to my alarm ringing. As I walk down-stairs, I'm still thinking about the dream. "The glove can take you there," I mutter as I pour cereal into a bowl.

"What was that?" Dad asks from the kitchen table.

"Nothing," I say.

"You ready for day two of grade three?!?" He asks with too much enthusiasm for first thing in the morning.

"I guess."

"I can't hear you. Are you ready for day two of grade three?!?" He asks this loudly. I guess he's trying to pump me up.

"I guess!" I shout.

"Woo! It's gonna be a great day, Kiddo!"

"Yeah, okay, whatever." My dad is so weird.

"Woo! It *will* be a great day!" Mom walks into the room, holding Lana.

As I take my bowl of cereal and sit on the couch in the living room, I continue to think about how weird my parents are. But I also think about the dream. It felt so real. I've got to tell the crew about it.

I get ready for school and head to the bus. Olivia is already at the bus stop when I arrive.

"Good Morning!" she says brightly.

"Hey."

"Ready for day two of grade three? It's gonna be a great day. Woo!" Geez, I feel like there's a contagious enthusiasm virus going around.

"I guess." I give her the same boring answer I gave my parents.

Hudson is saving a spot on the bus, and so is Ruby. Olivia sits down next to Ruby and I sit next to Hudson.

"I have to tell you about the dream I had last night," Hudson says.

"Me too. You go first."

"It was about the glove. In the dream, this guy in a wizard hat showed up."

Whoa. Creepy. "Weird!" I say. "That happened in my dream, too! Did he say something to you?"

"Yeah."

"Did he say something about going to another dimension?"

"How did you know that? That's so creepy." Hudson looks as surprised as I feel.

"I had the same dream!"

Olivia is listening in from across the aisle. "You guys had the same dream?" We tell Olivia and Ruby about what happened after they left the park, and about the dreams.

As we get off the bus and walk toward school, Ruby says, "We have to try it."

"Try what?" I ask.

"To use the magic glove to go to another dimension."

My heart is racing. Part of me is thinking there's no way this would work. But part of me is excited that maybe it *could*. "Should we try it today? Meet at Zombie Park again after a snack?"

"Yes!" Ruby exclaims. "All in favor say 'aye.'"

"Aye."

"Aye."

"Aye."

We reach the hallway where Hudson has to go to his classroom. "See you later," he tells us. He and I do our special high five. This one is my favorite. We raise our hands high and high five, then swing our arms down, turn around, and high five again behind our backs.

Mr. Watkins is wearing a red bow tie today. "Welcome to day two!" he shouts as he reaches his hand up for each of us to give him a high five.

We walk to our lockers. "Now we just have to figure out which dimension to tell the glove to take us to," Ruby says. "Think of some ideas and we'll talk them over at recess."

I sit down at my desk and start thinking about this. A candy dimension? No, too sticky. A dinosaur dimension? No, too deadly. This might take a while…

The Glove

2

Olivia brings a notebook and pencil to recess. She writes down our ideas for dimensions.

"How about an animal dimension?" Hudson asks.

"Or a comic book dimension!" I say.

Olivia writes these down and then looks up with her pencil raised. "A book dimension!" She quickly puts her pencil on the paper to write that down.

Ruby gasps like she always does when she has a brilliant idea. "A dimension where everyone is named Ruby!" she shouts.

"That might be confusing, but okay," Olivia says as she writes it down.

By the time the bell rings for lunch, we have a long list but haven't agreed on the dimension to choose. Hudson washes his hands with us in the wash fountain outside of the bathrooms, but he has to go to his class table to eat.

Olivia, Ruby, and I continue to think of ideas as we eat lunch. "How about a Lego dimension?" Olivia suggests, taking a bite of her pasta.

Darnell is sitting next to Ruby. "Why are you guys talking about dimensions?" he asks.

"We found a magic glove that will take us to another dimension," Ruby replies.

I can tell by the look on Darnell's face that he thinks she's crazy. "Um," I stammer. "Not really! We're just helping Hudson with a story for his class. We're all in the story and he's imagining we go to different dimensions."

"Oh, okay. You should go to a music dimension," he says.

"What would that be like?" Olivia asks.

"Probably like a musical. People don't really talk, they sing. And they don't really walk, they dance."

"Do you think there's a dimension where it's always lunchtime?" I ask.

"Oh, there's a dimension for everything," Ruby answers. "There's even a dimension where I'm president."

"What would that be like?" Olivia asks.

"A lot like the dimension where it's always lunchtime," Ruby replies.

I laugh and move my peas around my plate with my spoon, not really wanting to eat them. "In the dimension where I'm president, vegetables taste like candy."

We clear our trays and line up to go back to our classroom. I really want school to be over because I know the sooner it is, the sooner we can try out the magic glove. Ruby feels the same way. I know this because, on our walk back to the classroom, she says, "I wish school was over so we could try out the magic glove."

"Let's just try to have fun with our subjects this afternoon," Olivia says. "Time always goes faster when you're having fun."

We sit down at our desks and I try hard to listen and learn for the rest of the school day. I even have a bit of fun when Mr. Watkins tells us a joke. "Are monsters good at math?" He looks at me when he asks this.

"No?" I respond uncertainly.

"Not unless you Count Dracula!"

I laugh because it's a pretty funny joke. I'll have to tell my dad that one tonight. Dad loves jokes.

We get through math, and word study, and writing in our planner. "It's almost time!" I say to Olivia as we grab our things from the locker.

"You're really excited, huh?" she asks.

"Yeah! We're going to go to another dimension soon!" I'm surprised she's not more excited.

"You do realize we're just pretending, right?"

"No. I really think this is going to work. I mean, Hudson and I had the *same* dream."

"That's just a coincidence. It will be fun to pretend we're in another dimension, but don't get your hopes up about it actually happening." As she says this, Ruby joins us and we start walking to the bus.

"You're wrong, Olivia," says Ruby. "This is going to work. Roller coaster dimension, here we come!"

Hudson joins us and we get on the bus. Olivia sits next to me. I ask, "you really don't think it's going to work?" I was convinced it would, and I'm disappointed she doesn't think so.

"Just don't get your hopes up, Sawyer. Magic isn't real. However, we can use our imaginations and enjoy pretending."

I look out the window for the rest of the way. When Ruby gets up to leave, she tells us, "Four-thirty. Zombie Park. Bring the glove. Leave your backpacks at home. We don't want them to weigh us down."

When I get home, I say hi to Mom and grab some crackers for snacking. I still feel a little sad about what Olivia said. "Oh well," I mumble to myself. "She's right; it will be fun just to pretend." I grab my scooter, and Olivia joins me on the way to the park.

Hudson is there with Liz. I lean my scooter against the "for sale" sign of the house next to the park. Hudson pulls the glove out of his back pocket as we approach.

"Here, Olivia," he says, handing her the glove. "You try it on."

Olivia puts it on. "Weird," she says. "It has thermal capabilities. I wonder where that comes from." She takes the glove off and inspects it, flipping it inside out.

"Crew!" We hear someone shout. We look up to see Ruby running toward us. "Finally! I've been waiting for this moment all day!" When she reaches us, she leans over to catch her breath. "I...can't...wait..."

"What—" I start to say, but she holds up a finger to stop me.

"Don't… interrupt… me," she pants. When she can breathe again and talk normally, she says, "I can't wait to try the glove!" We all stare at her, not sure if she's done talking and not wanting to interrupt. "Okay. I'm done. You can talk now."

We have Ruby try the glove on. After a moment, during which her eyes widened and her smile grew, she takes it off and says, "This is definitely a magic glove."

"Did you feel the warmth?" Hudson asks. Ruby nods, still smiling.

"Who's going to wear it when we go to another dimension?" I ask.

"Hudson found it. I think he should wear it," Olivia says.

"Okay," says Hudson. He puts the glove on again. I wonder which dimension he's going to choose. We put so many of them on our list. "How do you think we do it?" Hudson asks, staring at the glove and twisting his wrist side to side.

Ruby responds, "If only *you* have the glove on, we probably all have to be connected to you; like holding hands, or putting our hands on each other's shoulders."

"And maybe just say out loud where you want the glove to take us?" I add.

Liz comes over with a stick, wanting to play fetch. Hudson takes the stick and throws it as far as he can. He looks at us. "Everyone put your hands on each other's shoulders." We do that. "Magic glove, take us to a sports dimension."

Immediately, I know this is a magic glove, after-all. I'd been hoping that it would *really* send us to another dimension. I don't know what I was expecting to happen — but it was nothing like what happened next.

Time for an activity! What are your ideas for dimensions? List them here.

The Sports Dimension (3)

It's like we're sucked into a swirling tunnel. I feel funny, like I can feel the millions of tiny feet of thousands of caterpillars crawling all over my body. I look at Hudson, Ruby, and Olivia next to me. Ruby and Hudson's eyes are wide and they're looking all around. Olivia looks worried. Dazzling colors and shapes swirl around us, like what I once saw looking through a kaleidoscope. We're moving fast, until we seem to fall out of the tunnel. I look up to see the colorful tube that we fell through. I only see it for a second, and then it's like the passageway closes and is replaced by a gray, domed ceiling.

We land on crunchy green turf. The first thing I hear when we land is a kid's voice, "Think fast!" I do not think fast. A football hits me in the face. Man, too bad

you don't acquire new skills when you go to another dimension. I could really use some athletic abilities.

The crew and I take our hands off of each other's shoulders and look at the kid who told me to think fast. He looks like he's about our age, but he looks different. He has purple skin and spiky yellow hair. "Hi. I'm Alex," he says. He comes up to me with his hand out like he's going to shake hands, but, instead of shaking my hand when I put it out, he slides his hand across it and up to my elbow. I guess this is how they shake hands in the Sports Dimension. He then does this same greeting with the rest of the crew. Ruby is last and she adds a twirl to the greeting. "You guys are new here, huh?"

"Yep," Ruby happily says. "Can you show us around?"

"Sure. This," Alex gestures his hand toward the area in front of us, "is the Football Wing." We look at it. It's huge! At least twenty football fields are in front of us. They're different from what we're used to, though. One of the fields is made of a bunch of trampolines. On another, all of the players are wearing jet packs. On another, the goalposts sit on top of a remote-controlled car that keeps moving. "Let's check out the other wings."

I follow Alex, along with the rest of the crew. As we walk through two huge blue doors with a sign on them that says *Aquatic Wing,* I think about how cool it is that he just welcomed us and is acting like it isn't weird that four kids he's never seen just dropped down into his football wing. I mean, if that had happened to me, I would have been pretty freaked out. "You're really nice," I say to him.

"Well, I wouldn't want other dimensions to think the Sports Dimension isn't a cool place," he responds. "You all look like you came from the Earth Dimension. Is that right?"

"How do you know that?"

"I've met other Earthlings. One of them was always wearing a glove like that," Alex nods toward the glove on Hudson's hand. "Do you guys know Bryce?"

I shake my head no, and so does the rest of the crew. I look around at the aquatic wing. There are many pools in front of us, including a huge one where the swimmers are racing on animals that look a lot like dolphins.

"Do you know Bryce's last name?" I ask.

Alex leads us back out of the blue doors and to a set of white doors with a sign that says, *Volleyball Wing*. "What's a last name?" he asks.

"We have those on Earth. My first name is Sawyer, and my last name is Andrews." I look around at the volleyball wing. There are many volleyball courts. A ball comes soaring toward us. Ruby catches it.

"Good catch," says a deep voice. I look around to see where the voice came from. Ruby screams and drops the ball to the floor.

"What's wrong?" Olivia asks.

Ruby looks up at her, her eyes wide with surprise. "The ball just *talked* to me!"

Alex reaches down and picks the ball up. "Who's the new girl?" the ball asks. "She seems rude."

I look at the ball and I see that it has eyes, a pouting mouth, and a brow wrinkled in a frown. I've never seen anything like it. "Sorry," I stammer. "We're new here."

Alex throws the ball back to a volleyball player. "Don't you have talking balls on Earth?" He asks us.

"No," Ruby says. "Isn't it weird to hit or throw something that talks?"

"Nah, they like it. Sometimes when we're done playing, they beg us not to stop. Or the mean ones yell at us." Alex leads us out of the Volleyball Wing and to another set of doors. These ones are orange and the sign says *Basketball Wing*. Hudson's jaw drops as we walk through the wing. I can understand why. One of the basketball courts has a shrinking hoop. In another, the players sit in the pouch of an animal that looks similar to a kangaroo. In another, all of the players are on stilts.

We walk through the Soccer Wing next, where one of the fields has an invisible ball. As we're leaving, Olivia hangs back. She has a worried look on her face. "What's wrong?" I ask.

"We've been here a long time. We need to get back. What if our parents have noticed we're gone and they're looking for us?"

I'd been so distracted that I hadn't even thought about this. "Guys!" I yell to Ruby and Hudson. They stop and look back at us, and so does Alex. "We should get back. We've been here a long time."

Hudson nods. "You're right." He looks down at his glove. "Hopefully getting back is as easy as getting here."

"Oh, it is," Alex says. "I saw Bryce do it lots of times. You just have to tell the magic glove to take you to the Earth Dimension. But, come on, let me show you one more wing. This one is my favorite of all."

Ruby and Hudson start to follow Alex. I want to follow him, too. The rest of the wings were so cool, and this one must be amazing, considering it's Alex's favorite. Olivia still looks worried, and she hasn't budged. "Come on," I beg her. "Let's just look at one more. I promise we'll go back after this one."

Olivia hesitates but says okay. We follow Alex through two huge black doors. There, I see what might be the most fun-looking place I've ever seen. In front of us are obstacle courses. Every kind of obstacle course you can think of — like ninja warrior courses, inflatable obstacle courses, aerial obstacle courses, and more.

"Hi, Alex!" yells a girl at the obstacle course that is closest to us. She has purple skin and long orange hair. She's standing next to a table with a bunch of bottles on it. Some of the bottles are short, some are long. Some are skinny, some are wide. All of the bottles are different colors. "You want to race?"

"Not right now, Giselle. I'm showing these new kids around."

"Okay. Hi, new kids!" Giselle picks up a short bottle with a black letter on it. She takes a drink of it. She puts it back on the table. Then something really strange happens. Her body changes. It gets wider, and shorter, and *hairier.* Giselle turns into a gorilla! I'm stunned as she then races through the obstacle course. When she gets to the finish line, she transforms back into her old self.

"What just happened?" asks Ruby.

"Don't you have potions that transform you into animals on Earth?" Alex asks.

"No."

"Oh. Earth is so weird."

"Okay, this has been fun," says Olivia, "and thanks very much for showing us around, Alex, but we need to get back."

"I understand. I hope to see you again soon." Alex then puts his hand out and does his hand sliding thing up to Olivia's elbow. He does this with the rest of the crew, too.

Hudson looks a little nervously at Alex. "So I just tell the magic glove to take us back?"

"Yep, but say it confidently. You are the boss of that glove and you need to declare where to go."

"Okay," says Hudson. He doesn't sound confident. "Everyone put your hands on each other's shoulders again."

As we put our hands on each other's shoulders, I start to worry. What if our parents *are* looking for us? What happens if Hudson doesn't say it confidently? What if we don't make it back?

Hudson's voice breaks my thoughts. "Magic glove, take us back to the Earth Dimension."

It's time to use your imagination and help illustrate this story! Draw a sports wing that you'd like to visit.

Wizard Dream (4)

The world around us starts to swirl and we get sucked into another twisting, colorful tube. I feel the million caterpillar legs again. We keep our hands on each other's shoulders until we stop.

The first thing I see is Liz. She's running. She jumps and catches a stick in her mouth.

Ruby's also watching Liz. She looks around. "Who threw that stick to her?"

I look around Zombie Park. It's deserted.

"Hudson, you threw a stick for Liz to fetch before we left, right?" Olivia asks.

"Yeah," Hudson says as Liz runs back to him with the stick and drops it at his feet. He picks it up. "Do you think that was from when I threw it?"

Olivia looks at Ruby. "What time does your watch say?"

Ruby looks down at her watch. "Four forty."

"But it felt like we were in the Sports Dimension for at least an hour," Hudson says. "The next time we go, let's set a timer when we get there and see how much time it actually is. Time must be different there. It was only seconds here from when I threw the stick and when Liz caught it."

Ruby reaches for the glove. "Let's go again! I want to check out a food dimension."

Olivia grabs her hand. "No way! Once a day is enough. In fact, I'm not sure we should ever do that again."

"Why not?"

"It could be dangerous! We need to tell an adult about this."

I think about this. "I don't think an adult would believe us."

"Well, then we'll just have to show them."

I realize Olivia is right. Dimension travel might not be safe. "Which adult do we tell?"

"How about your mom, Sawyer?" Hudson suggests.

"Okay."

"Make sure you tell her tonight," Ruby says. "I really want to go to the Food Dimension tomorrow."

"Okay," I say again. We play fetch and run around with Liz for a while until Ruby's watch alarm chimes.

"I gotta get to soccer practice," she says.

"Have fun," Hudson says.

"I feel like soccer will never be the same after seeing how they do it in the Sports Dimension. I mean, where's the challenge when you can actually *see* the ball?" She waves goodbye and walks toward her house.

"So what are you going to say to your mom?" Olivia asks me.

"I guess I'll just tell her the truth."

Hudson scratches his head. "That will be an interesting conversation, 'hey mom, we found a glove at the park and it has a wizard hat on it and it makes you feel warm and it can transport you to another dimension.'"

41

Olivia tilts her head to the side like she always does when she's thinking hard. "This is probably something we have to show her, not just tell her about."

I realize she's right. No adult would believe this unless they see it for themselves. "I'll go talk to her now."

"We'll come, too," Hudson says. He pulls Liz's dog leash off of the picnic table that it had been sitting on and clips it back to Liz's collar loop. Olivia and I grab our scooters and we start riding to my house.

My house isn't big, but it has a great sledding hill in the backyard. The house is blue with a yellow door. We open the front door to the hallway and I peek into mom's office to see if she's still working. She isn't in there. "Sawyer, is that you?" I hear her call from the kitchen.

"Yeah, mom," I say. "Olivia and Hudson are with me." We walk into the kitchen. My mom is chopping up a cucumber.

"Hi, Olivia and Hudson," she says cheerily.

"Hi, Mrs. Andrews."

"Did you all have fun at the park?"

"Yes, we did. Mom, there's something I want to talk with you about."

Mom must have heard the seriousness in my tone. Her face gets serious, too. She puts the knife down and steps away from the counter and toward me. "What is it?" she asks. She sounds a little scared.

"Well," I start, and then gulp. "I wanted to let you know. We found something at the park. It's a glove with a wizard hat on it. And Mom, it's magical. It took us to another dimension."

Mom's face relaxes and she steps back to the knife and cucumber. She starts cutting it again. "Oh, okay. What was this other dimension like?"

"It was a sports dimension. There were all these cool football fields and stuff."

"Oh, that's nice," she says. She starts putting the cucumber pieces in a Tupperware.

That was too easy, I think as Olivia, Hudson, and I exchange glances.

Olivia asks, "Mrs. Andrews, can we show you what it's like? We can take you to the Sports Dimension."

Mom looks at Olivia and smiles. "Well, I'm getting dinner ready right now. Lana and Sawyer's dad will be home soon."

"Don't worry. Time is different there, so it will be like hardly any time passed here on Earth."

Mom looks at the clock on the wall. She shrugs her shoulder. "Sure. Why not?"

Hudson pulls out the glove and puts it on. "Okay, we all have to put our hands on each other's shoulders."

Mom smiles, but I can tell she doesn't believe anything is going to happen. She thinks we're just kids playing pretend. We all put our hands on each other's shoulders.

"Magic glove," Hudson says. "Take us to the Sports Dimension."

I take a deep breath, waiting for the swirling tunnel to begin. But it doesn't. We're still standing in my kitchen, hands on each other's shoulders.

Hudson clears his throat. "Magic glove, take us to the Sports Dimension!" This time he says it sternly and louder.

Nothing happens.

Mom takes her hands off our shoulders. She looks around the kitchen with a wondrous look on her face. "Wow! You're right. There are football fields, so many of them. Look, that one has a pink ball!" She points at the fridge. She's humoring us. "That's incredible, kids! But I really need to get back to making dinner.

Sawyer, we'll be eating in thirty minutes. You can hang out with your friends until then." Mom goes back to the counter. "You kids have fun!"

"It didn't work," Hudson says as we walk back to the front hallway, then go outside. "Why didn't it work?"

We sit down in the front yard. Olivia and Hudson seem to be lost in thought, just like me. Why *didn't* it work? Maybe the glove only works once? Maybe since Ruby was with us the first time, she always has to be with us for it to work?

"Maybe it can't work if you're inside a house?" Hudson suggests.

Olivia's head is tilted. "There could be a lot of reasons it didn't work. It could be something about the situation, the location, the people involved, lots of things. My hypothesis is that it didn't work because your mom is an adult. Maybe her mind is too closed to the concept and so it doesn't work for her."

"But you didn't think it was going to work, and it still did when you were with us," I respond. I remember how disappointed I felt when she told me that magic isn't real.

"Well," Olivia takes a deep breath. "I felt different-ly once I tried the glove on and felt that warm feeling spread over me. There wasn't a logical explanation for it, so I started to think it *was* magical."

"Should we test your theory?" Hudson asks.

"How?"

"We could bring another kid with us next time. Maybe one of your brothers."

Olivia has two little brothers. One of them is in first grade, the other is in preschool.

Olivia tilts her head again. "I think there are still too many uncertainties for me to agree to that. What if something happened to them?"

"Okay," Hudson says. "Well, let's see what Ruby thinks about this tomorrow. I need to get home. I'll see you guys tomorrow." He grabs Liz's leash and high fives me. Olivia high fives me and grabs her scooter.

"See you tomorrow," she says.

"Sounds good." As she rides away and Hudson is pulled down the road by Liz, I see Dad's car coming. He pulls into the driveway and garage. I walk over and open Lana's door.

"Soy-ya!" she yells. She can't pronounce my name right yet. She grins at me as I unclip her car seat. Once I've picked her up, she gives me a big hug. For a second, I think maybe we should try to take Lana to another dimension to test Olivia's theory. Then I think about what she said about something happening to her brothers and I know we shouldn't try it with Lana. I couldn't stand it if something happened to her. If only we had someone we could ask about traveling to other dimensions, someone who could teach us more about how it works…

After dinner, we play a family game of charades. Then it's the same bedtime routine. As Dad tucks me in, I ask, "Dad, what do you do if you want to learn more about something but you don't know how to learn about it?"

Dad fluffs my pillow. "I'd probably just do an internet search."

I hadn't thought of that. "Good idea. Thanks, Dad."

"Sure thing, Son. See you in the morning." He shuts my light off and closes my door.

That night I dream I'm back at Zombie Park with the crew. I put the magic glove on and feel the same warm feeling flood over my body.

"Hey," Hudson says, pointing behind me. "It's the man in the wizard hat!"

We all turn and see the man standing a few feet away from us.

"Hello," the man says. "I see you found the glove."

"Does the glove belong to you?" Olivia asks.

"It did. Not anymore though. Now, it belongs to you kids."

"Why didn't it work when we tried it with my mom?" I ask.

"It doesn't work on those who don't believe."

"I knew it!" cries Olivia.

Before we can ask more, I wake up. My room is still dark. I look at my alarm clock. It's three in the morning, but I don't feel tired. I walk downstairs to get a drink. I gulp down a glass of water and put the cup down on the desk in our kitchen, right next to the family laptop. I remember what Dad said about doing an internet search, so I log on to the computer. I go to a search engine and type *Magic glove*. Lots of things come up, but nothing useful. *Glove with a wizard hat on it*, I try. Again, a lot comes up, but nothing helpful. I shut the computer off and go back upstairs to bed. As I fall back to sleep, I hope the wizard joins the dream again so I can ask more questions.

I wake up to the sun streaming through my window. I try to remember if I had any more dreams after I went back to bed, but nothing comes to mind. Later, as I pour my cereal I wonder, did Hudson have the same dream as me again?

Slam Dunk

On the bus, I sit next to Hudson and we both ask in unison:

"Did you dream about the wizard guy last night?"

"Yes!"

Olivia is listening in from the seat across the aisle. "I did, too!" she whispers.

Hudson describes his dream, and it's the same as Olivia's and mine. "The dream answered our question," he says. We turn to Ruby in the seat behind us and look expectantly at her.

"What you looking at me for? I dreamt that I saved the city from giant slugs." Then she gasps. "Maybe that dream answers a question for us, too."

"What question would that be?" asks Olivia.

"*Can* Ruby save the city from giant slugs? Oh yes, she can." Ruby looks up from her seat. We'd just stopped at a bus stop and a stout kid with thick eyebrows is walking up the bus stairs. "Who's that kid?"

I watch as he walks down the bus aisle. He stops a few seats in front of us where Ruby's younger brother, Tony, is sitting at the edge of the seat. The new kid says something to Tony and Tony gets up quickly and sits in the seat in front of me. Tony is at the edge of the seat and he looks sad. He's just a kindergartener so he's usually more sensitive than us third graders. "What's wrong?" I ask him. "What did he say to you?"

Tony looks up at me. There are tears in his blue eyes and his lips are quivering. "He said, 'You're in my seat.'" A tear slips down onto his freckled cheek and he quickly wipes it away.

Ruby shoots up in her seat. "Hey, new kid!" she yells angrily.

The rest of the bus gets quiet, and heads turn.

The new kid looks back. "Are you talking to me?" he asks.

I stand up, too. "Yeah, she's talking to you," I say. I'm surprised at how confident my voice sounds. My heart is racing. "What are you doing picking on a kindergartner?"

The bus slows, pulls into the lot in front of our school, and comes to a stop. The bus driver stands up and looks back at us. "What's going on back there?"

Olivia stands up. She yells, too, but doesn't sound at all mad. "Bill, this kid kicked a kindergartner out of his seat. It was mean, and not fair."

Bill the bus driver looks at the new kid. "Is that true?"

The new kid hesitates. "No," he lies.

"It better not be," Bill says. "There are plenty of seats to go around." All of us kids are frozen and quiet in our seats, but then he gestures to the door. "Alright, everyone get to school." The noise of chatter returns, and kids file off the bus.

Tony gets off the bus right in front of me. I put my arm around his shoulder. "I'll walk you to your class this morning, Buddy." If I were a little kindergartner and a big kid was just mean to me, I'd want someone to walk me to class.

Ruby gets off the bus behind us, along with the rest of the crew. "Where'd he go?" she asks, craning her neck to look over the crowd of kids.

I look around. He must have run ahead of us, and it's impossible to find the back of his head amongst the many others. "I don't know. I don't see him."

"Do you think he's a third-grader, too?" Hudson asks as we start walking.

"He looked older," Olivia says.

The kindergarten classrooms are on the way to the third-grade ones, so the whole crew and I walk Tony to his classroom door. I keep my arm around his shoulders. "Don't let that kid get to you," I say. "He was being a bully, and that's never okay." He looks at me and his face doesn't look sad anymore. He actually gives me a little smile.

We each give Tony a high five and walk to our third-grade hallway. We say bye to Hudson. As we walk into the room, Ruby cheers, "yes!" I see she's looking at the whiteboard that has our schedule for today on it. "Phy ed class!" she says.

I don't share her enthusiasm. If I could list my favorite specialist classes, it would be: 1. Computer, 2. Art, 3. Library, 4. Music, and — in very last place — 5. Phy ed class. I mean, occasionally we'll do something fun like play with the big colorful parachute or play on scooters, but most of the time it involves playing a sport, and sports are just not my thing.

I groan when we get to phy ed class because Mr. Kodiak explains we'll be playing basketball. If I could list my favorite sports, it would be: 1. Bowling, 2. Pool (except when I hit the eight ball in accidentally), 3. Darts, then a whole bunch of other sports, and then basketball last.

"We'll start by practicing dribbling," Mr. Kodiak says. He demonstrates, and he doesn't even hit the ball off of his shoe once. He's obviously better at it than I am. "I'm going to partner you up. You and your partner will share a ball. One of you will practice dribbling, then I'll blow the whistle and the other will practice dribbling."

I get partnered up with Ruby. She grabs a ball from the bin. "I'll go first!" She starts dribbling. Ruby has always been good at sports, but today she is like really, really good. She dribbles the ball under her legs. She does a figure eight dribble around her legs. Darnell's ball rolls our way and she scoops that up and starts dribbling two balls at once.

"Hey, give me my ball back," Darnell says. While still dribbling one ball, Ruby throws Darnell's back to him. Darnell catches it but continues to watch Ruby. "Wow, you look like a pro!" he says. Ruby dribbles the ball, while running, to the hoop. She does a lay-up and the ball swooshes through the hoop.

"Wow!" Mr. Kodiak calls from across the room. "That was awesome, Ruby, but we're not shooting yet." He blows the whistle and everyone passes their ball to their partner. Ruby does a chest pass hard to me, and *then,* and then I actually *catch the ball.* I'm excited and also surprised. By the look on Ruby's face, so is she. I start to dribble and it feels easy. It feels smooth.

"Have you been practicing?" Ruby asks.

"No." I wonder if I could dribble the ball in between my legs like Ruby did. I take a deep breath and suddenly it's like my hands move without my telling them what to do! I easily bounce the ball between my legs like a pro.

"Good job!" Ruby says. "You should try to figure eight the ball."

Can I do that? I feel like I can. I try it, and then I do it *twice.* I grin at Ruby, "How am I doing this?"

"Try to make a shot!" she replies.

"But Mr. Kodiak said we're not doing that yet!"

"Just tell him you forgot. Come on. Try it!"

I can't help myself. I run to the hoop, dribbling the whole way. I jump toward the hoop, and here's where it gets really strange, I *reach the hoop*. I jump *that high*. At that point, easy peezy, I just set the ball into the hoop and gravity brings me down. I watch my feet land back on the ground, and I look up. Everyone in the phy ed class is frozen and staring at me. I'm surprised like they are, but I decide to play it cool. "What? Haven't you ever seen a third grader do a slam dunk?"

Mr. Kodiak is close by. He shakes his head to get the stunned look off of his face. "Uh, no," he replies. "No, I've never  seen a third grader do a slam dunk. You must have practiced really hard this summer. Did you have a personal basketball coach?"

"No."

"Okay, well, it wasn't time for shooting, so you should have waited. However," he looks around the phy ed class and raises his voice, "*now* it is time to practice shooting. One of you will shoot while the other is the rebounder, then I'll blow my whistle and you'll switch." He pauses and looks at me, then yells again, "and we're just doing regular, non-slam dunk shots. I don't want anyone getting hurt."

Ruby goes first, and she makes every shot. It's easy for me to rebound for her. Somehow, I can tell as the ball starts to come down exactly where it's going to land.

"That slam dunk was awesome!" Olivia says. She throws a ball to Darnell. "Why do you think you're so good all of a sudden?"

"What? Like I wasn't good before?"

She looks at me, the kind of look that says *are you kidding me?*

"Okay, you're right," I say to her. "I wasn't good before. Maybe my muscles grew. I did take a drink of my dad's protein shake yesterday."

Mr. Kodiak blows his whistle and Olivia and I catch our basketballs and move to shooting. We both easily make our shot.

"I don't think one drink of a protein shake can make you this good," she replies. "And have you noticed? Ruby and I are playing really well today, too." She catches the ball when Darnell passes it to her. "Think about this: what dimension did we visit yesterday?"

"The Sports Dimension."

"And what are we suddenly really good at?"

"Sports."

"This can't be a coincidence."

I catch the ball as Ruby throws it to me. I shoot it. Again, I make the shot. Olivia is right. The only explanation for this is the fact that we were in the Sports Dimension yesterday. I have so many questions! Will this last forever? Does this happen in every dimension? Will Hudson be like this, too?

As phy ed class ends and we return the basketballs to the bins, I also think about how I really want to go to a dimension where everyone is a millionaire.

Make a list of your favorite classes and your favorite phy ed activities.

Alex's Dad

"I vote we go to Zombie Park ASAP today," Ruby says as we sit down on the bus at the end of the day. "Drop off your school backpack, grab your Zombie Park backpack, grab a snack to-go and your water bottle, and I'll see you there."

"I need to bring Liz, too," Hudson says. We found out on the way to the bus that Hudson had serious basketball skills in phy ed class today, too. He made every shot. Mr. Kodiak even asked him to demonstrate a proper lay-up for the class. "What dimension are we going to visit today?" he asks.

"It's my turn to choose," Ruby says. "We're going to a food dimension."

I don't know why Ruby thinks it's her turn. Hudson picked the dimension yesterday, but Olivia and I haven't had a chance either. "Why isn't it Olivia's turn?"

Ruby looks at me like I'm crazy, but before she can say anything, Olivia says, "It's okay. Ruby can take a turn next."

"Or Sawyer could," Hudson replies.

Olivia shrugs her shoulders and looks at me. "If you could choose a dimension, which would you choose?"

I pause to think, and an idea hits me. Alex! He knew about dimension travel. He's our best shot at learning more about it. "I'd go back to the Sports Dimension."

"Boring!" Ruby says. "We need to check out somewhere new."

"I want to go back to the Sports Dimension because Alex is there," I say. "He knew we were from Earth, and he knew about dimensions. I think he could answer some of the questions we have."

"Good point. Okay, we're going back there to talk with Alex." Hudson looks at Ruby as he says this.

Ruby crosses her arms. "A food dimension will be more fun, and we can talk with Alex another time.

Let's take a vote. Who wants to go back to the Sports Dimension that we've already seen?"

"Aye," I say.

"Aye," Hudson says.

We look at Olivia. Her head is tilted. She looks from Ruby to me, and back to Ruby. "Sawyer does have a good point that Alex might answer our questions." Ruby's jaw drops. "*However*, once we get back, I think we might also be able to go to the Food Dimension to-day."

Ruby's face changes from mad to grinning. "Okay. That works for me."

When we get to our stop and exit the bus, Olivia and I run to our houses. I swing open the door, drop my backpack, and run to the kitchen. Mom is loading the dishwasher. "Hi, Mom!" I open the pantry door and grab a granola bar. I start to run out of the kitchen.

"Hold on, Pal," Mom says. I freeze and turn around. "I need your help loading this dishwasher."

"But, Mom," I groan. "The crew is waiting for me at the park."

"It will only take five minutes." Mom hands me a dirty plate and I realize there's no point arguing. I grab the plate and put it into the bottom rack of the dish-washer. "How was your day?" Mom asks.

"Great! We played basketball in phy ed class and I played really well." Mom hands me a bowl and I load it into the dishwasher.

"That's great! Did you make any shots?" She hands me a stack of cups and I load them.

"Yes, a bunch of them." Mom hands me a cup filled with silverware and I load them into the silverware compartment.

"Very cool. I finished that work project I was telling you about today, and my boss had really nice things to say about it." Mom starts wiping down the sink. Yes! That means there are no more dishes. I finish loading the silverware.

"Can I go now?" I ask excitedly.

Mom nods. "Wash your hands, and then, yes, you may go. Thanks for helping."

"Yep!" I say, already running up the stairs. I wash my hands. I grab my Zombie Park backpack, then my scooter, and head to the park. I notice the "for sale" sign that I've been leaning my scooter on is gone, so I lean it on a tree.

"What took you so long?" Ruby calls.

"I had to help my mom load the dishwasher." Liz drops a ball in front of me and I throw it for her. She races after it. "Is Olivia here yet?"

Hudson nods toward the curve in the road. "Not yet, but I see her now."

Olivia is walking toward us but is still a couple of blocks away. "Hurry up!" Ruby calls. Sometimes I feel like Ruby is rude. Like the time the zipper on my pants was down last year during recess. She could have just told me quietly about it. Instead, she stood up on the playground equipment and yelled, "Everyone! I have an announcement!" She waited for everyone to be quiet and look at her, and then she pointed at me and yelled, "Forget something?" followed by, "His undies have hearts on them!" I was so embarrassed. My mom had given me heart undies for Valentine's Day.

When Olivia gets to the park, she's out of breath because she listened to Ruby and went as fast as she could. Hudson pulls out the glove and hands it to Olivia. She takes it and takes a deep breath. She looks around at all of us. "So, we're going back to the Sports Dimension?"

We all nod.

"Yep!" says Hudson.

We put our hands on each other's shoulders.

"Magic glove, take us to the Sports Dimension!"

The swirling starts and we all smile at one another. Ruby starts yelling, "Wooooo!" We land in the same spot we did last time, overlooking the Football Wing.

"We made it!" says Olivia. She looks down at her watch and hits buttons on the screen. "I'm starting my timer."

We walk around, stopping to watch a play on the trampoline field and the jet-pack field.

"I wonder where Alex is," I say, looking about us.

As I say this, a man with yellow skin and orange hair walks by and gives us a confused look. Maybe he's never seen Earthlings before.

"Did you say you're looking for Alex?" he asks.

"Yes."

"He's at our house, resting. He's sick."

"At *our* house? Do you live with Alex?" I ask.

"Yep. I'm his dad."

"It's nice to meet you," Olivia says. "Do you think we could visit Alex?"

"I don't think so, kids. He's really sick. I wouldn't want you to catch what he has."

"What does he have?" Ruby asks.

His dad gives us a sad look. "Poor guy has the football pox."

"Do you mean the chickenpox?" Hudson asks.

"No, that's what you have in the Earth Dimension. Here we have the football pox. We get spots on our bodies, too, but they're in the shape of a football. And they're not itchy like the chickenpox. Instead, they're cold. It feels like someone has placed an ice cube on your skin where each of the spots is."

Poor Alex! That sounds miserable. "We definitely don't want to catch that," I say. "Maybe we can come back another day. When do you think he'll be better?"

"This usually lasts a week. But can I help you kids with something? Are you lost?"

The crew and I look at one another. Do we bother trying to explain to an adult why we're here? We tried telling mom about this and she didn't believe us. But Alex's dad did mention the Earth Dimension, so he must know something about this dimension traveling thing. "Well, like you said, we're from the Earth Dimension," I say. Alex's dad nods. "We're new to traveling to other dimensions, and we wanted to learn more about it."

"Well, then you came to the right place."

"You know about dimension travel?" Olivia asks.

"Know about it? I don't just know about it, I helped *discover* it."

I can't believe our luck! I look at the crew and they look just as excited as I am.

"Tell us everything!" Ruby says.

"Well, it's a long story. But, don't worry, I have a way to teach you everything you need to know. Follow me to my lab." He walks out of the Football Wing and into the hallway. We follow him past many doors with signs on them like *Bowling Wing* (I really want to go in that one), *Tennis Wing*, *Rugby Wing*, and more. Finally, we get to an area that looks like a waiting room. There are chairs, and a big front desk, and lots of windows. Through the windows, I can see a world that looks similar to ours on Earth, but also very, very different.

Andrew's Lab

The first thing I notice when we walk out of the building is that the ground is *blue*. But what's even more weird is that when Alex's dad steps on it, he *bounces*. The ground is made out of rubber, or something a lot like it. And when he steps on it, he bounces high. He turns in the air and calls back to us, "I know this is different from Earth, but you'll get used to it."

Ruby is the first to follow, then Hudson, then me, then Olivia, each of us stepping and bouncing. It's like the ground is a giant trampoline. As I bounce, I stop and look around. The colors here are very different. The trees are stretched, and they swirl at the top. Most of the buildings are so high that the tops fade into the sky. I look back at the building that we came from and am surprised to see the face of a dragon underneath the door that we'd come out of. The dragon's eyes are closed and small puffs of smoke are occasionally coming out of its nose. "Is that a dragon?" I ask, my eyes wide.

Alex's dad looks back at us as he lands on the ground, flexes his legs, and bounces again. "Yes. That's a Giant Many-Winged Dragon. They're very rare."

Olivia's jaw is dropped. "You have dragons here?"

"Yes, of course. That's what each of our sports lands - the Football *Wing*, the Volleyball *Wing*, and so on - are on top of. Each sport land is on top of a dragon wing."

"Uhh.... what happens when the dragon wakes up?" I ask nervously as I bounce next to Alex's dad.

Alex's dad shakes his head. "Well, lucky for us the Giant Many-Winged Dragon sleeps for hundreds of years at a time. However, when he wakes up, it's a lot like what you in the Earth Dimension call an earthquake. I'm proud to say I came up with a machine many years ago that can predict when the Giant Many-Winged Dragon is going to wake, and I can say with utmost certainty that this one won't wake up for at least another four hundred years." He gestures with his hand. "Now, come on. Let's get to the lab before the precipitation hour." He turns and bounces forward, and we all follow.

"What's precipitation hour?" Olivia yells.

"Oh, right, you don't have that in the Earth Dimension. Every afternoon here there's an hour of precipitation."

Ruby grabs Olivia's hand as they bounce forward while holding hands. "Wow, you mean it rains or snows for an entire hour?"

"Maybe. It depends on the clouds. Sometimes it's rain, sometimes it's snow, sometimes it's bouncy balls or ping pong balls."

As we bounce past a fountain with a statue of a fisherman, Alex's dad says, "There's the lab, just ahead." Ahead of us is a small brick building with a domed roof. Alex's dad continues, "Since you're new to this, you should crouch on your final bounce to stop. Watch me demonstrate." As he gets to the building, he crouches down. His hands hit the rubbery ground and he grips it with them.

We follow and do the same. My hands squeeze the ground. It feels like squeezing a stress ball. I'm still now. I stand up.

The brick building has a domed roof and a purple door. The door swings open and a cloud of teal-colored smoke billows out. A woman wearing safety glasses, gloves, and a lab coat steps out. She looks at Alex's dad. "Andrew!"

Alex's dad, who I guess is named Andrew, waves his hand in front of his face as the smoke spreads around him. He coughs. "Gina, I told you not to mix up the trial monkey formula without me."

Gina looks embarrassed. "Sorry. I was hoping to perfect it before the obstacle animal dash this weekend." She turns to go back into the building. When she does, I notice a long, thin, curling tail dangling below her lab coat.

Andrew notices the tail too. "Oh, boy. Looks like the mix worked, at least partly!" He looks at us. "Don't worry. It's always temporary."

Gina is opening up the windows from the inside. More teal-colored smoke billows from them.

"Now isn't the best time for us to go into the lab," Andrew says. He leans down like he's going to bounce away, then stops. "Unless any of you could use a temporary monkey tail." He looks curiously at us.

Before the rest of us can respond, Ruby shouts, "Yes!"

I cover up Ruby's mouth before she can say more. "No, no need for a monkey tail. Thanks! Can you tell us more about how the dimension travel works without us going in your lab?"

Andrew taps a finger on his chin. "Hmm, actually, I can. Hey, Gina!"

Gina pops her head out of a window. Her ears are now round and sticking out from her head like a monkey. "What can I do for you, Boss?"

"Please go in the watch cabinet and pull out one of the boxes labeled 'Dimension Travel X3.' "

"Sure thing, Boss," Gina says and disappears from the window.

Olivia looks down at her watch. "Guys, we should probably get back soon."

Gina comes out and hands a box to Andrew. He opens it and pulls out a watch. He looks at our wrists. I'm the only one not already wearing a watch. He steps toward me and I hold out my arm. He puts the watch on me.

"This is one of the Dimension Travel X3 watches. I invented it myself as my team and I were discovering and exploring dimensional travel." He holds down a button on the side of the watch and the watch's screen lights up. He looks at us. "What questions do you have about dimension travel?"

We all look at each other. There are hundreds of questions going through my head.

"Why couldn't Sawyer's mom travel to another dimension?" Hudson asks.

"X3," Andrew calls. "Tell us why Sawyer's mom couldn't travel to another dimension."

A male voice comes from the watch. "I don't know who Sawyer's mom is, but generally dimensional travel does not work for someone if they have no faith that it will work. It will also not work if the person does not possess the strength and energy to make the trip."

"There you go," Andrew says. We hear a loud crack and he looks up to the sky. "Uh oh, the precipitation hour is about to start!" He puts his hands over his head and an orange ping pong ball bounces off of it. "You all should go. Take the watch with you. It will answer your questions."

Ping pong balls start falling from the sky like a torrential downpour. "Put your hands on each other's shoulders!" Hudson has to yell this because the sound of ping pong balls hitting the ground and the trees and the buildings is *loud*. We do as he says and Olivia must have told the magic glove to leave because suddenly we're back in the swirling, colorful tube.

It's time to use your imagination and help illustrate this story! Draw the crew at Andrew's Lab.

The Food Dimension ⑧

When we land, I look around at Zombie Park. Our world looks so dull compared to the vibrant colors we'd just seen in the Sports Dimension. It also seems boring considering it never rains ping pong balls. I wonder if they make ping pong angels instead of snow angels there.

"Okay, time for the Food Dimension!" Ruby says. She reaches her hand out to Olivia. Olivia takes off the glove and hands it to Ruby. Ruby puts it on.

"Oh!" Olivia looks down at her watch. "According to my timer, we were in the Sports Dimension for one hour and four minutes."

Hudson looks at the watch on his wrist. "But my watch says it's only four forty. So time definitely moves slower here." We all nod. He pets Liz and throws her ball. "Maybe next we could go to an animal dimension."

"No time to talk. Everyone put your hands on each other's shoulders," Ruby states.

As I put my hand on Hudson and Ruby's shoulders, I see a pine cone hit the ground in the middle of our circle. I feel something hit my back, and look over at Hudson to see a pine cone hit his back. I keep my hands on their shoulders but look around. "The pine cone thrower is back!"

Ruby speaks before anyone can respond. "Magic glove, take us to a food dimension!"

The swirling tube appears, but this time it's not as colorful. It's black with specks of white light. And we're in the tube longer this time. I look at my friends. Ruby is grinning from ear to ear. Hudson also looks happy. Olivia looks worried. "What's taking so long?" she asks.

We land. But we're not on land. We're in outer space, surrounded by stars and darkness. I look down. Hudson and I have landed on a skylight window. The skylight window is on top of a big, hard, dark green spaceship. I wonder why we aren't gasping for breath. I know astronauts have to wear oxygen tanks in space. This dimension must be different. Suddenly I'm falling through the skylight window, and so is Hudson. We land with a thud on the soft, green floor of the spaceship. I look up. Olivia and Ruby are peeking down into the hole left by the skylight window collapsing.

"Are you guys okay?" Olivia calls down.

I reach down so I can use my hands to stand up. The floor of the spaceship sticks to me. "We're fine, but this floor is gross."

I hear a deep voice to my right. "Hey! I don't come to your dimension and insult your floors!"

My body freezes and Hudson and I look at each other with wide eyes. Who made that sound? He sounds mean. And big. I look toward the direction of the voice and see the front windows of the spaceship. Through the windows is the big, expansive darkness of space and stars. In front of the window are control panels filled with buttons and levers and blinking lights of all colors. In front of the controls are two big, dark purple chairs. The chairs are turned toward the controls so I can't see who's sitting in them.

Hudson speaks quietly to me. "Ruby did say 'food dimension', right?" I nod. He continues, "then why are we in a spaceship?"

I shrug my shoulders, look up, and wonder if I should gesture for Ruby and Olivia to jump down. But then I think that, if the owner of the deep voice is as mean and big as he sounds, they may be safer up there.

The owner of the deep, mean voice clears his throat. "You folks going to introduce yourselves, or what?" Hudson and I step toward the voice and one of the chairs swings around. "I hope you don't think you can just break someone's skylight and not at least introduce yourselves."

When I see the owner of the deep, mean voice, I almost laugh. Sitting in the chair, which, as I step closer, I realize looks like an eggplant, is a creature that looks like a bunny. He has long bunny ears, cute dark eyes, and whiskers. However, he doesn't have fur. Or a body, either. He looks like he's made out of french fries.

"Hi. I'm Sawyer, and this is Hudson," I say. I reach my hand out to shake his paw.

"I'm Brian," he says. He reaches his paw out, but before he and I can shake, an alarm sounds. Brian turns toward the controls. "We've got an incoming! You, Sapien…"

"Sawyer," I correct him.

"Whatever, Kid, just sit down in the other chair and take hold of the orange lever."

I sit down in front of the control panels and notice there are four orange levers in front of me. "Which orange lever do I grab?"

"The orange one!" Brian says. He jerks the steering wheel (which looks like it's made out of licorice) to

the right. The spaceship turns sharply in the direction of the wheel. "You need to pull it *now*!" he demands. "Pull the orange lever!"

"There are four orange ones!"

"No, there aren't. One is apricot, one is ginger, one is honey, and the other one is *orange*! Stop wasting my time and pull the orange lever!"

I look at Brian, and then I look out of the front window to see a big, round, red object coming slowly toward us. I look down at the levers and guess at the different colors, pulling the one that I think is the most like orange. The spaceship shakes and I see an orange object emerge from below the front window and shoot toward the big red object that is coming toward us. I keep watching and realize the orange object that was shot out of our spaceship is a carrot. Then I realize what the big red object is.

"Is that a giant *tomato spaceship*?"

Brian the french fry bunny is frantically pushing control buttons. He moves a lever and we start backing away from the approaching spaceship. I see a small explosion of red sauce as the carrot impacts the tomato spaceship. "Yes, it's a giant tomato spaceship. But not just any giant tomato spaceship. It's from the fleet of the coyotes, our greatest enemy."

"Uh, Sawyer," Olivia says from behind me. I turn my chair around to look at her. She and Ruby must have jumped down from the top of the spaceship. "Hudson and I agree that we should go back to our dimension. This food dimension seems too dangerous."

"But I think we should stay here and shoot as many carrots as we can!" Ruby says enthusiastically.

"Well, if you're going to do that, now is the time," says Brian. "Because the coyotes just shot a cucumber torpedo back at us."

A cucumber torpedo? I wonder how big it is and how badly it will damage this spaceship. My heart starts to race. "I'm with Hudson and Olivia! We should go back home," I say quickly. I look from Ruby to Brian and realize he may need help. "It seems like we came at a bad time. Do you want to come with us to Earth, Brian?" I ask, standing up and taking hold of Olivia and Ruby's shoulders. Olivia takes hold of Hudson's shoulder.

"No way. My avocado spaceship is a thousand times stronger than their tomato one. I got this. Eat carrots, you lousy coyotes!" he screams as he launches another round of missiles.

"Yeah, a real bad time," I mutter.

"Brace for impact!"

"Get us out of here, Ruby!" Olivia yells.

"Magic glove, takes us back to the Earth Dimension!" Ruby says and back into the black tube we go.

Lasagna ⑨

When we land, Liz runs over to greet us. She wags her tail as Hudson pets her head. "Well that was not what I was expecting when I thought of a food dimension," he says.

I nod. I'd been picturing marshmallow clouds and houses made out of crackers, not spaceships and torpedoes.

Olivia sits down in the grass and looks around at us. "That was dangerous. We could have gotten hurt."

"I don't know about that," Hudson says. "We don't really know how this works. Maybe you can't get hurt in a dimension that isn't yours. Like you're protected."

I remember that I'm wearing a watch that is supposed to answer our questions about dimension travel. "X3," I say. "Can a person get hurt in a dimension that isn't their own?"

The watch lights up and the voice says, "Usually not. When you travel through the tunnel that brings you to another dimension, the tunnel prepares you for the dimension to come. It assesses the properties of the area you're coming from and the area you're going, scans you for needs, and equips your body to withstand any threats in the environment you are about to land in."

Ruby grins at me and looks down at the watch. "X3, does that mean we're invincible in other dimensions?"

"Almost," X3 responds.

Olivia sighs and stands up. "That makes me feel a lot better."

I reach over and put my arm around Olivia and squeeze her shoulder. Sometimes I wish Olivia didn't worry as much as she does. She worries about getting good grades, not getting hurt, making sure the people around her aren't fighting, basically everything.

Ruby interrupts my thoughts. "Let's go to another dimension now!"

I guess it's good that Olivia worries, because her cautious nature is a good balance with Ruby's recklessness. Ruby doesn't think before just plunging ahead with something. "I've had enough dimension travel for today," I say. "Let's play here in the park for a while and ask X3 more questions." I look around and lower my voice. "Also, the pine cone thrower was here before we left. He must still be around."

Ruby runs toward the rock-climbing wall. She looks behind it and must not see anything because she keeps running around the park. As she runs back to us, she yells, "I don't see anyone!"

Hudson kneels down next to Liz. "Liz, did you see who threw the pine cone, girl?" Liz barks quietly and jogs toward the woods. Liz is a really smart dog. She understands English; she just can't speak it.

We follow her to the woods, but Olivia stops when we get a few feet in. "I'm not supposed to go further."

Hudson and I stop next to her, but Ruby keeps jogging behind Liz. "No one will know! Come on. We need to find the pine cone thrower."

I don't want to go further, so I'm happy when Hudson calls, "Liz! Come back, girl!" Liz turns around and trots back to Hudson, her tongue dangling out of her mouth.

Ruby continues jogging into the woods.

"Ruby!" I call after her. "Let's ask the watch more questions!" She stops and looks back at us. I start to walk toward the playground. Hudson and Olivia join me.

"Wait up!" Ruby calls. We turn back around and Ruby is jogging toward us. It isn't long before she's right next to us. "X3!" Ruby says. My watch lights up. "What is the coolest dimension?"

"The coolest dimension is the Frozen Dimension," the watch responds.

"No, I mean what is the most awesome dimension?"

The watch doesn't light up or respond.

"You have to start with 'X3'," Olivia says. "X3, what is the most awesome dimension?"

It responds this time, "The Most Awesome Dimension is located in the Blue Limestone galaxy. The population of the Most Awesome Dimension is five thousand twenty-two stonelidites..."

"That doesn't sound so awesome," Ruby interrupts the watch. "X3, what is the dimension that people like to travel to the most?"

The watch lights up. "The Earth Dimension is the most highly rated place for dimension travel."

Really? I feel like Earth is boring compared to places like the Sports Dimension. "X3, why is Earth the most highly rated place for dimension travel?" I ask.

The watch lights up. "According to reviews, travelers enjoy the diverse populations on Earth of people, plants, and animals. They also like the YouTube videos."

We all laugh.

Ruby takes the glove off and hands it to me. "You should choose for us to go to a chemistry dimension next!"

I put the glove in my pocket and shrug my shoulders. I can think of several dimensions I'd like to visit, but a chemistry one isn't on my list. "I need to think about it."

"I can bring the list of dimension ideas that we'd come up with tomorrow," Olivia says. "I need to get home and start working on my homework, though."

I'd forgotten Mr. Watkins had assigned homework to us tonight. "I better go, too." I do my special high fives with Ruby and Hudson and grab my scooter. I decide to carry it so Olivia and I can walk together.

"So, do you think we acquired any skills from the Food Dimension?" Olivia asks.

I think about how good at basketball I was, thanks to the Sports Dimension. What would the Food Dimension make me good at? Eating? Cooking? Shooting torpedoes at a giant tomato? I shrug. "I don't know." I remember the watch and look down. "X3," the watch lights up. "Why were we good at basketball after visiting the Sports Dimension?"

"In some dimensions, travelers temporarily obtain abilities that are necessary or common in that dimension," X3 responds.

Olivia speaks up. "X3, do travelers to the Food Dimension obtain any temporary abilities?"

"Travelers can obtain different types of abilities and different levels of abilities in dimensions. In the Food Dimension, it is common to come back knowing new recipes."

"Well that doesn't seem very useful," I say. My stomach rumbles and I wonder if Mom or Dad have picked out what we're having for dinner already. If not, I think I'll whip up a nice lasagna.

We reach Olivia's house. "See you tomorrow." We high five, and then I ride my scooter the rest of the way home.

"Mom!" I yell when I get inside. I put my Zombie Park backpack down.

"Hi, Sawyer," Mom calls. I follow the voice and find her putting together a cabinet. "This cabinet for the loft was delivered today." She pauses and picks up the electric drill, drilling a screw into the cabinet.

"That's cool, Mom." My stomach rumbles again and I swear it sounds like it's saying *lasagna*. Without thinking, I say, "Do you know if we have Italian sausage, ground beef, onion, garlic, tomatoes, basil leaves, Italian seasoning, parsley, lasagna noodles, ricotta cheese, mozzarella cheese, parmesan cheese, and an egg?"

Mom blinks a couple of times. "Um, we have about half of those things. Are you craving lasagna?"

"Yes, and I want to make it myself."

"Ummmm… that's great. Your dad and I would love some help In the kitchen." Her phone chimes and she looks down at it. "And you're in luck. Your dad just sent me a text to say he's stopping at the grocery store. I'll let him know you want to make lasagna and have him pick up what you need."

Yes! "Thanks, Mom. You're the best!"

"No problem. Now I need your help." She hands a door for the cabinet to me. "Hold that steady right there while I drill in the screw." I do what she asks and she drills in the screw. "Do you have homework tonight?"

"Yes."

"Why don't you get it done now, then you can cook when Dad gets home?"

"Okay." I go downstairs and grab my homework from my backpack. It's math, but it's not too hard. I finish it in no time and return it to my backpack. I grab a cookbook from a shelf in the kitchen and start looking through it. I think about how these recipes could be so much better. I grab a pencil and start adding ingredients to each recipe.

Lana and Dad come home. "Good to see you, Sawyer!" Dad says. "Please get your shoes on. I could use some help carrying the groceries in."

Lana runs to me and reaches her arms up toward me. "Hug first! Hug first!" I hug her, then put my shoes on and help Dad carry the bags of groceries in. I start opening the lasagna ingredients.

I've never done anything like what happens next. As I go to work on the lasagna, it's as if my hands have a mind of their own. I watch as they set the water for boiling and slice the sausage. Dad offers to help, but I wave him away. My hands  dice the vegetables, grate the cheese, and crack the egg all without thinking about it. I almost feel like a puppet - and I don't know who's pulling the strings!

An hour later, my lasagna is ready. Dad pulls it out of the oven for me. "It smells so good!" He puts it on the counter. "We just need to let it cool down."

I'm at the counter, mixing up a corn side dish. "Sounds great! If Lana is hungry, I cut up some berries. She could eat them while we wait for the lasagna to cool."

"Oh — okay," Dad stutters a little.

Lana comes over and pulls on Dad's pant leg. "Lana hungry!" Dad scoops her up and sets her on a chair. He grabs the berries from the fridge and puts them in front of her.

Dad turns to me. "Sawyer," he says. "Is there a reason you're suddenly interested in cooking? Are they teaching about that at school?" Mom comes into the room and gives Dad a hug.

"No," I shrug. "I guess I just wanted to give it a try."

"Well, that's wonderful!" Mom says. "It smells so yummy. I think we're going to have a great night!"

I smile at my family and think it's going to be a great night, too.

The Robot Dimension

10

The next day at school is boring, except for phy ed class, during which the crew and I made all of our basketball shots again. I wonder how long we'll keep our new skills. We meet at Zombie Park after school. It's my turn to choose a dimension. Olivia brings the list that we'd written down and hands it to me. "Wouldn't it be fun to go to a library world?" she says. "Just an idea."

"That sounds about as fun as getting a flu shot," Ruby replies. "Let's go to a Ruby dimension!"

I look over the list and decide on where I want to go. I'm already wearing the glove. "Okay. Everyone put your hands on each other's shoulders." After everyone is linked, I say, "Magic glove, take us to a robot dimension!"

The world around us starts to swirl and we get sucked into a swirling, silver, metallic tube. I'm not surprised to feel the caterpillar legs again. I've been thinking of what a robot dimension would be like. My guess is robots will do all the hard stuff — cleaning, cooking, homework - and people will just get to play and have fun.

We come out of the tunnel and land on a concrete floor in a deserted hallway. A door to our right opens and a short balding man walks out. He's hunched over and holding his stomach. "Thank goodness you guys are here," he says. He wipes sweat off of his forehead. "My family and I, we're all sick. We need someone to substitute for us."

"Substitute?" I ask. If this guy thinks we're going to be substitute teachers, some students are about to have a very long recess. Well, except for the class Olivia substitutes for. They'll probably read at least four chapter books today.

"Yes, substitute. This speech is critical for winning the election. We've got twenty thousand robot people out there. Can you hear them?"

When he pauses, I listen closely and I do hear the sound of a crowd. I wonder what robot people are.

"Come on, I'll take you to the suit." He pauses for a second, wipes the sweat off his brow again, and takes a deep breath. We follow him down the hallway. "This suit is state-of-the-art," he says with pride. "It took five years to perfect." He opens a big metal door and we walk into a dark room. "Lights on!" The lights turn on. "Here he is." He stretches out his hand and pats a big piece of metal. "I call him T and he's four times the size of the most common robot suits. Entry for the head is here." He taps the metal and a door on the side of the robot's head opens. I look inside and see a chair with a screen in front of it.

As we walk along the length of the great suit, the man taps again on the arm of the robot. Another door opens. "Here's the entry for the arm controls."

I'm impressed by the size of this robot. It's about as big as my house! "How big is T?" I ask.

"He's about thirty gearies." I'm not sure what a "gearie" is. Is it like the size of my ruler? The man taps on the middle of the robot. "Here are the controls for the torso." He moves on and taps on the leg of the robot. "And, last but not least, the controls for the legs and feet." He clutches his stomach and wipes sweat off his brow. He reaches his hand into the pocket of his shirt and pulls out notecards. "The speech is written on these cards," he grunts.

"So, you want us to control this robot suit, and read your speech to *twenty thousand* robot people?" I ask.

"Yes, exactly." He holds the notecards out toward me, but I don't take them.

"We're just kids. Isn't there someone else who can do this?"

"No. There's no one else. The speech was supposed to start ten minutes ago, and the crowd is already getting antsy. No one in my family is well enough to do this. And you aren't just kids. You're dimension travelers. Everyone knows dimension travelers are brave." He holds out the notecards again, this time to Olivia. Olivia takes them. "The speaker will be in the head of the robot." He walks Olivia back to the head.

"Are we really going to do this?" Hudson asks through gritted teeth.

"Yes!" Ruby says. "You heard him. He needs us, and we're brave. This will be easy." She walks away and gets into the door that controls the arms of the robot.

"Ruby is probably right," I say. "There were only like three notecards in his pocket, so the speech isn't even long. And I've always wanted to control a robot." I smile at Hudson and pat him on the arm. Then I step into the door of the torso of the robot and sit in the chair. A seatbelt automatically wraps around me.

The man leans in through the door. "What's your name, Kid?"

"Sawyer."

"Okay, Sawyer. The screen in front of you has everything you need. It's also equipped with the latest voice technology. If you want the robot to twist the waist of its body, just tell it to do that." He opens a drawer and pulls out a black headset. "You can also talk with your friends using this headset." He hands the headset to me and I put it on my head. "I'll get your friend settled into the leg, and then open the warehouse door. He'll control the feet to bring you right onto the stage. Then Olivia can read the speech into the microphone, Ruby will wave at the crowd, and you'll bring the robot back in."

"Okay," I say. The man shuts the door and walks away. "Hello?" I say into the headset.

"Hi, Sawyer!" Ruby says. "I was just telling Olivia she should talk about giving out free donuts if we're elected. Who wouldn't vote for someone who gives out free donuts?"

"I'm just going to stick to what's on the notecards, Ruby," Olivia replies. "This seems pretty easy to control, huh?"

I look at the screen in front of me. There are just three buttons on the screen. I hit a button that says *camera view* and see the ceiling of the warehouse. I realize this is a view of what the robot's eyes would see. "Yeah, seems easy." The picture on the screen in front of me brightens as the man opens the warehouse door to the outside. The sound of the crowd gets much louder. They're chanting, "T for president! T for president!"

"Okay," I hear Hudson's voice. I can hear him take a deep breath. "I'm going to make T stand and walk onto the stage."

It's a good thing I have a seatbelt on because things get very shaky as the robot stands up and steps forward. On the screen, I see a tall microphone on a stage. Below the stage stands robot after robot, stretching as far as I can see. None of them are as big as the robot we're in. Many of them are raising a mechanical fist in the air as they chant. "T for president!"

"Wow! That's a lot of robots," I say.

"What?" Ruby asks. "You're breaking up."

"I said, 'that's a lot of robots!'"

The crowd quiets down as Hudson brings T up to the microphone.

Through the corner of my eye, I see something white falling inside of the robot. "Oh no!" Olivia says. "I dropped my notecards."

"I caught them," Hudson calls. "I … them … you … read …"

"You're breaking up, Hudson," I say. "We can't understand you." The crowd is getting louder again. They sound impatient.

"I'll read them to you, Olivia," Hudson says, loud and clear.

"… good… repeat … crowd." Oh, geez. Now Olivia is breaking up.

Hudson starts reading the notecards. "Hellooooo, robots!"

Olivia repeats this into the microphone, "Hellooooo, robots!" The crowd cheers loudly.

"We need a president who cares about fellow robot people!" Hudson reads. Olivia repeats this and the crowd cheers loudly again.

"… need … president … sure … hungry." Oh, no. Hudson is breaking up again.

"What?" Olivia asks quietly. I wonder if the robot people can hear her.

"… need .. president … sure … hungry," Hudson repeats.

"Uh, we need a president who makes sure no robot person is hungry!" Olivia yells. The crowd cheers.

" … need … president … strength … metal … human…"

"Hudson, I can't make out what you're saying," Olivia whispers. "Uh…" She leans into the microphone. "We need a president who cares about the strength of our metal as much as the strength of our human bodies!" The crowd must have liked hearing this, because they erupt with cheers, and start chanting again.

Once it's quieter again, Hudson reads, "we … run … bananas … gears…"

I have no idea what Hudson was trying to say. "Hudson, can you repeat that?"

"We … run … ba-nanas … gears…"

Olivia clears her throat. "We will run with bananas and gears in our hands!" she shouts. The crowd doesn't cheer this  time. They just stare at T. Then they look at one another. It feels awkward. As the seconds tick by, I think Olivia must have said the wrong thing. Then a red robot in the front steps forward and turns toward the crowd.

"With bananas and gears in our hands!" he chants.

The green robot next to him also steps forward and turns toward the crowd and joins the chant. "With bananas and gears in our hands!"

Soon there are thousands of robots chanting this. They cheer louder when Ruby raises T's arms in triumph, and then waves goodbye. Hudson turns the feet back toward the warehouse door, walks us in, and we use our screens to lay the robot back down. I take off my headset, open the door, and step back onto the concrete. The rest of the crew joins me.

"We will run with bananas and gears in our hands?" Hudson asks Olivia.

"It was impossible to hear what you were saying!" Olivia says defensively. "I made a guess." Hudson hands the notecard to her and she reads it. "'We will never run out of bananas or gears again.' Oops."

"Oh, well. I guess it worked out. They seemed pretty happy," I say.

Ruby grins and claps her hands. "Let's go out there again. This time I want to make the speech!"

"I think that was enough speeches for today," says the man. He's clutching his stomach again, and his face looks green. "Thank you for stepping in. I don't know what we would have done if you all hadn't been in the hallway. Had we canceled the speech, we'd never win the election."

"You're welcome," Olivia says. "I hope you and your family are feeling better soon." She turns to me. "We should get back."

I nod and we put our hands on one another's shoulders. "Magic glove, take us back to Earth."

We travel back through the metallic tube and land at Zombie Park.

Ruby pulls the glove off of my hand. "Whose turn is it next?"

"Hudson's," I say. Ruby looks disappointed. I think she was hoping I'd say her name. She hands the glove to Hudson.

Hudson looks at Olivia. "I think Olivia should go again."

"No, that's okay. I'll wait," Olivia responds.

"Olivia, take a turn, and choose an adventure dimension!" Ruby says.

"Um, okay," Olivia says. We put our hands on each other's shoulders. "Magic glove, take us to an adventure dimension!"

We get sucked into the swirling tube. This time it's green and brown and very windy. The wind is hurting my eyes so I close them. I struggle to hold tight to Olivia's shoulder and I can feel Hudson's shoulder slip from my grip. When I open my eyes, we're not in the tube anymore. I glance at Olivia, then look around for Hudson and Ruby. I don't see them. "Where are Hudson and Ruby?"

Olivia's eyes are wide and tears are welling in them. "We lost them!"

"What?"

"We lost them in the tube. They're not here."

It's time to use your imagination and help illustrate this story! Draw T speaking to the crowd.

Transformation Soda ⑪

My first thought is that Olivia must be joking. But then I remember that Olivia isn't really the joking type. "You're kidding, right?"

Olivia's lower lip quivers. "No. We lost them." Her voice cracks and a tear slips down her cheek.

"Maybe we didn't lose them. Maybe they just landed somewhere else." I look around. We're on a deserted beach. Small waves are sweeping onto the sand in front of us. Behind us is a bunch of palm trees. I start walking toward the trees and gesture for Olivia to follow me. I cup my hands over my mouth and yell, "Ruby! Hudson!" Olivia follows me and yells their names, too. I can see far, but I don't see anything but palm trees. I stop and grab my water bottle from the side of my Zombie Park backpack. I take a drink. "How is this an adventure dimension? It seems boring to me."

"I'd rather it be boring than dangerous," Olivia replies. She takes a drink from her water bottle too, then we walk more. "What are we going to do? How are we going to find them?"

We reach a break in the palm trees and there are mountains in front of us. I nod toward them. "Maybe they landed up there." I really think they have to be here. I mean, Olivia told the glove to bring us all to an adventure dimension.

"X3," I hear Olivia call. My watch lights up. "Are Ruby and Hudson here in this dimension with us?"

"I'm sorry. I don't know that," the watch responds.

"X3, what happens if dimension travelers separate during travel?"

The X3 watch responds, "What happens if dimension travelers separate during travel depends on when they separate. If they separate in the travel tube, the travelers likely end up in different dimensions."

I think about what this means. Ruby and Hudson may be in a different dimension, and Olivia is the one wearing the glove. How are they going to get out of that dimension?

Suddenly, the ground below me starts to shake. I hear Olivia gasp. "Look!" She points behind me. I turn and see smoke and some kind of blue ooze spilling out of the top of the mountain. I realize it's not a mountain - it's a volcano!

"I don't know what that blue gunk pouring out of there is, but it's flowing toward us!" Olivia looks at me. "What do we do?"

I think about our options. We could try to climb a palm tree.
We could run into the ocean. We could try to climb one of these other mountains. But wait, what if they also are vol-canoes that are going to erupt?

Before I can make up my mind, Olivia yells, "Run!" We run away from the blue liquid and into the barren area between the mountains and the palm trees. I look back and see the liquid is getting closer, oozing around the trunks of palm trees. Then something to my left catches my eye: a rope ladder dangles from a palm tree!

"Olivia!" She looks back at me. I grab her hand and run toward the rope ladder. She trips and falls. "Come on!" I reach down and pull her up.

"Ow!" She's keeping her left foot up. She must have hurt it.

"We have to hurry!" I put her arm around my shoulder and help her hop to the rope ladder. I get on first and climb up several steps. I reach down and help her climb, too.

"Ow, ow, ow," she says as she climbs. At the top of the ladder, hidden by the tree's leaves, we find a tree-house. Below us, the blue liquid flows around the bottom of the rope ladder. Olivia points back to where the volcano was. "Look!"

The volcano is gone. In its place is a waterfall. All of the mountains are gone, replaced by a river. The palm trees are gone, too. Instead, there are deciduous and coniferous trees like we have in my neighborhood. Even the palm tree we climbed a moment ago has changed into an oak tree!

Olivia touches a branch above her head. "It's like whatever that liquid was washed away one land and made it into another!" She sits down, takes off her backpack, and un-zips it. "I have a first aid kit in here." She digs through the bag until she finds a small red box that looks like a briefcase. She opens it and pulls out a bag that says *instant cold pack* on it. She squeezes it, then puts it around her ankle.

"Does it hurt really bad?"

"Yes." She gulps. "I'm not worried about myself, though. We have to find Ruby and Hudson." She puts her foot up on her backpack. I take another drink of my water. Suddenly, Olivia gasps and sits up. "I know! Let's just put our hands on each other's shoulders and tell the glove to take us to the dimension that Ruby and Hudson are in!"

Why didn't I think of that? I sit down next to Olivia and put my arm around her. "Wait — what about your ankle?"

"There will be time enough for that once we find Ruby and Hudson," she says as she puts the first aid kit back in her backpack. She puts her backpack back on and her arm around me. "Okay, here we go: magic glove, take us to the dimension that Ruby and Hudson are in!"

I wait for the swirling tube to surround us. It doesn't. We look around us, then at each other. "Why isn't it working?" I ask.

Olivia shakes her head. "I don't know."

I look down at my watch. "X3, why can't we leave the Adventure Dimension?"

"Generally dimension travel does not work for someone if they have no faith that it will work, or if they don't possess the strength and energy to make the trip."

Strength and energy, I think. Maybe Olivia can't travel right now because she's hurt! Olivia strokes her hands on the ice pack. I think she's thinking the same thing I am. Then her head jerks toward the rope ladder. "Did you hear that?"

I hadn't heard anything, but now I listen more closely. It sounds like people laughing. I look down at the river and see two kids walking alongside it. One of them, the boy, looks up at me and stops walking. The girl notices he stopped and follows his gaze. They smile at each other and run toward the base of the tree. "There's two kids down there," I tell Olivia. "They saw me and they're running over here."

"Do they look mad?"

"No, not at all. They look happy."

"Helloooo," I hear the girl cheerily call as she climbs up the rope ladder. When she gets to the platform of the treehouse, she gets to her feet and grins at us. Although she mostly looks like someone from Earth - she even has yellow rain boots like my mom - she has slits on her cheeks. *Are those gills?* I think about asking this but realize that might be rude. "Are you enjoying our treehouse?" she asks.

The boy gets to the top of the rope ladder and stands next to the girl. "Don't be rude, Vivian," he says. "Let's introduce ourselves." He waves at us, and I notice his fingers are webbed. "I'm Victor."

"I'm Sawyer, and this is Olivia."

Vivian crouches down next to Olivia and looks at her foot. "You're hurt!"

"Yeah. I hurt my ankle when we were running away from the ..." Olivia pauses, not knowing what to call whatever the liquid was.

"The transformation soda?" Vivian asks. Olivia nods. "You don't have to run from it. It doesn't change animals or people, just the landscape. If it touched you, you'd just get a little wet and sticky."

"We didn't know that," I say.

"Is it going to change again soon?" Olivia asks.

Vivian and Victor look at one another. Victor shrugs and Vivian walks over to the trunk of the oak tree. She pulls out a necklace from under her shirt. I can see it has a key hanging on it. She inserts the key into a key-shaped hole in the oak tree and a square-shaped compartment opens. Vivian pulls something out of the compartment and starts swiping on it with her finger, and I realize it's an electronic tablet.

"According to the transformation index, we won't have another transformation until Thursday. Ooo," she smiles at Victor. "It's going to be a floral landscape."

"Yes! We can fill the honey jars!" Victor looks at Olivia, then back at Vivian. "You should request a healer."

"Already doing that," Vivian replies as she swipes on the tablet again. "The earliest available one can get here in ninety wavutes."

"Is that a long time?" Olivia asks.

"Where are you guys from?"

"The Earth Dimension."

"You're dimension travelers? Awesome! We've heard about guys like you, but it's so cool to meet some in-person! I've always wanted to try it myself. Let me just convert wavutes to an Earth unit of measurement." Vivian pushes on the screen of her tablet. "It says ninety wavutes is about the same as ninety minutes on Earth."

"An hour and a half?" Olivia gives me a worried look. "That's a long time. A lot could happen to Hudson and Ruby in that time."

"Who are Hudson and Ruby?" Victor asks.

"They're our friends from Earth," I explain. "They were traveling with us and we lost them on the way."

Olivia tilts her head to the side. "Maybe you should try to find them without me, and then come back here when you do."

I think about this. I don't like the idea. I'm scared to travel around another dimension by myself. What if something happens and I can't get back to Olivia? I'm also worried about Ruby and Hudson, though. What if they're trapped in a dangerous dimension?

"Ooooo! Oooo, I have an idea!" Vivian says. She's jumping up and down and clapping her hands. "I'll travel with you to find your friends, and Victor can wait for the healer with Olivia. Then we'll bring everybody back here. The healer will make Olivia better and then we can have a deliverer bring us some delicious food!"

I do like delicious food. "What do you think of that plan?" I ask Olivia.

"I think that's our best option." Olivia takes the glove off and hands it to me.

I put the glove on. "Thanks."

"You're welcome." Olivia still looks worried. I wonder what she's thinking. Maybe she's worried I won't come back. Maybe she's worried that this land is dangerous. Maybe she's worried we won't find Ruby and Hudson. I feel bad that I'm taking the glove. I feel like I need to leave her with something. I take my X3 watch off and hand it to her. "Here. You keep this safe until I get back."

Olivia smiles a little and takes the watch. She already has a watch on, but she puts the X3 watch on, too. "Thanks."

I do my special high five with Olivia, then take a deep breath and look at Vivian. She has a huge grin on her face. She looks at Victor. "I can't wait to tell Mom and Dad about this!"

"They'll be so proud," Victor responds. He walks to the oak tree compartment and pulls out a backpack. "Take the adventure pack." Vivian puts it on her back.

"The glove will transport us both as long as we're touching," I say. She reaches her webbed hand out and I grab on to it. It feels a little strange, like holding hands with a duck, but that's okay. "Are you ready?" I ask her.

"Yes! I am SO ready!"

"Okay. Magic glove, take us to the dimension that Ruby and Hudson are in!"

The swirling tube is green and brown and windy again. I keep my eyes open this time though, and hold Vivian's hand tightly. We aren't in the tube long before we land. The ground is muddy and I hear a sound, like a bird squawking, in the distance. We're surrounded by huge trees.

"Look!" Vivian says, pointing through the trees.

What I see next makes me gasp. "Is that what I think it is?"

"Yep. *That* is a dinosaur."

Climbing Trees

12

The dinosaur has a long neck, a huge body, and thick stubby legs. I have a dinosaur book at home and I think this type is called a brachiosaurus. It's so big, but at least I know it's an herbivore. "I'm glad it won't eat us."

The ground shakes as the dinosaur takes a step in our direction. "It might not *eat* us," says Vivian as she turns and starts jogging away from the dinosaur. "But it could *step* on us!"

"Good point," I say and start jogging alongside her. "How are we going to find Ruby and Hudson?"

Vivian ducks under a tree branch and looks back. I look back too and realize the dinosaur isn't moving its

feet anymore. It's eating leaves off of a tree near where we landed. We stop. Vivian points at the muddy ground. "Footprints!"

I look down and see the footprints, too. Happiness bubbles up inside of me. They're not dinosaur prints. They're people prints! And they're the same size as my feet, which means they probably belong to Ruby and Hudson! I smile at Vivian and start following the tracks. "Hopefully they're still close!"

The trees are thick and there are a lot of branches and bushes so sometimes the footprints stop as we walk along, but it's pretty easy for us to find the tracks again. I continue to hear squawking in the distance. I wonder what kind of animal is making that noise. As I decide it's probably some sort of crow, we lose the footprints again. We walk around, trying to find where they start up again.

"I can't find any more," Vivian says, looking about.

"Let's look again." I concentrate on the ground, walking all over the area that the footprints had stopped.

Vivian walks around, too. She sighs. "I don't understand how the footprints could just stop. The ground is muddy everywhere. They should have continued."

I go back to where the footprints stop, right next to a tall tree. I look up at it. It's so high that I can't even see the top of it. It has lots of big branches, from bottom to top. Trees like this always make me think of Ruby because I know she wouldn't be able to resist climbing them. "That's it!"

"What?" Vivian asks. "Do you see your friends?"

"No, but I know where they went."

"Where?"

"My friend Ruby loves climbing trees. I'm sure she climbed this one."

Vivian looks up at the tree, too. "Do you think she's still up there? And what about Hudson?"

I think about this. Hudson doesn't like heights. Maybe Ruby talked him into climbing though. I put my hand on one branch and then step up onto another one. "Only one way to find out." I start to climb.

Vivian follows my lead. The tree is so big. It's tiring to climb it. Sweat starts to trickle down my forehead.

When we get to a huge branch about halfway up the tree, I climb onto it and sit down for a break. "Ruby! Hudson!" I yell as I look around. I don't see any movement, just many, many branches. I listen closely for them to call back. They don't. I pull a bag of sour candies out of my backpack and offer one to Vivian.

"What are those?"

"The best candy ever."

"You have shelser bites?"

Shelser bites? Must be something in their dimension. "Um, no. These are sour cirkells."

"Oh. I haven't had that before, but I'll try it." Vivian takes a candy from the bag, unwraps it, and puts it in her mouth. She makes a face like the one I made when I bit into a pizza my mom overcooked and burned. Vivian spits the candy out.

Then I hear a loud, long growl. I look down and see a very, very large dinosaur. It continues to growl and shake around its head. Vivian and I both have to grab onto the branch that we're sitting on because the dinosaur stumbles into the tree trunk and makes the branch shake. I'm happy we didn't stop climbing before this because we're just taller than he is.

"This one's not an herbivore," Vivian whispers to me, her violet eyes wide.

"I know," I whisper back.

"It's a..." Vivian gulps. "It's a T-rex!"

"I know that, too." As I'm looking down at the T-rex, I notice its eyes are closed. It stops stumbling around and starts to rub its face on the bottom of the tree trunk that we're on. Our tree is shaking so much that Vivian and I both have to lie down and grip the branch with our arms and legs.

"Do you think he knows we're up here and he's trying to shake us down?" Vivian whispers.

I look down at the T-rex and see it still hasn't opened its eyes. Then I realize one of his eyes is yellow. Wait, *is* that an eye? I squint my eyes and realize it isn't. It's the sour candy! It's stuck to his eyelid. He must be shaking his face against the tree to try to rub it off. "It's the candy," I whisper to Vivian.

"Huh?" She looks down and sees it. "Oh, wow. I guess I have good aim."

"No, you have bad aim. Like, *very* bad aim." My mind drifts back to Ruby and Hudson. "Do you think this is what happened to them, too?"

"I don't know. Does that happen a lot in your dimension? You all spit a lot of sour candies at dangerous animals? Is that like some sort of sport for you guys? I mean, I really like adventure, but that just seems dangerous."

"What? No. I didn't mean this *exact* situation happened to Ruby and Hudson, but maybe they climbed this tree, too, and something came along so they couldn't climb back down. Maybe this is like the T-rex's territory."

"Oh, maybe." The tree is still shaking. We're both hugging it hard, but it's still difficult to hold on. "Do you think we should climb up further, or do we just wait here until he leaves? What should we do?"

Before I can answer her, I lose my grip on the branch. I start to fall, hitting my arms and legs on branches on the way down. I land with a thump on the ground, right next to the T-rex's foot.

Flying?

13

The foot that I'm lying next to is bigger than my dad's car. It has sharp claws longer than my scooter. There is good news. First, I don't think the dinosaur heard my fall over the sound of his growling. The second piece of good news is that he stumbles away from me, still shaking his head and closing his eyes. The third piece of good news is that, although I'd gotten some scrapes as I hit the branches on the way down, I don't think I have any serious

injuries.

I'm not sure what to do. Do I try to run? Do I try to climb back up the tree? I look back up to the branch that Vivian is on. I can see she's standing up, then she's moving off of the branch. But she's not climbing down the tree. She's floating. Hmm, maybe she's not floating at all. Maybe the fall knocked me out and this is a dream. It does feel real though as she floats down toward me. I hear a snort from the dinosaur and what sounds like a sniff. I can't help but look over at him, and I realize he's gotten the sour candy off of his eye. My heart starts to race when I realize that eye is now looking right at me! He growls and runs toward me. He's just about upon me! But then, Vivian sweeps me off the ground, her arms under my armpits. We float back up, through the canopy of the tree, and into the sky.

"That was close!" Vivian says in my ear.

I can see everything up here! The treetops, a pond with all kinds of dinosaurs drinking out of it, and a white tree that's so tall it towers over the many others. I realize I've been holding my breath and I take a deep inhale. "You didn't tell me you could fly!"

"I can't fly."

"Well, in my dimension, we call this flying."

"Oh, in my dimension, we call it using a jet pack."

Jet pack? We've reached the white tree that towers over the others. Vivian lowers us onto one of its thick branches. I look behind her and see flames coming out of her backpack. Had she not just mentioned a jet pack, I would have thought her backpack was on fire.

"Adventure pack, shut off the jet pack," she says, and the fire goes out with a light pop and a small puff of smoke.

"You have a jet pack?"

"Umm, yeah," she says as if it's a stupid question and *everyone* has a jet pack.

"So we could have gotten away from that T-rex sooner?"

Vivian looks embarrassed. "Yes, I suppose we could have. Sorry."

"What else do you have in your adventure pack?"

"Lots." Vivian sets her backpack down on the branch and un-zips it. She digs through it. "Snacks, water, a tent, a first aid kit, thermal imaging goggles, all-purpose shoes."

"Wait. What's that?"

"All-purpose shoes. They're shoes that can fit anyone and can transform to suit any terrain. They can become rain boots, snow boots, ice skates, water skis, ..."

I feel like this list could get very long. "What about the thing before that, thermal imaging goggles?"

"Oh." She pulls out a pair of goggles and hands them to me. "Here, try them on and see for yourself."

I take them, stretch the strap over my head, and put the goggles in front of my eyes. The world in front of me changes. The plants, the sky, the pond all turn to shades of neon green. Vivian and the animals around the pond are bright yellow and red.

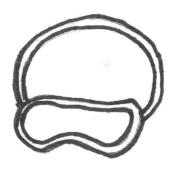

"The goggles detect heat. Animals are warmer than plants, so they stick out with the thermal imaging goggles," Vivian explains. "Hey! Maybe we can use those to find your friends." Vivian digs through her backpack again and pulls out a smaller backpack. "You can use the backup jet pack and I'll use the regular one. We can fly around and you can watch for your friends with the goggles."

I excitedly take the backup jet pack from her and put the straps around my arms. I loosen it so it hangs below my Zombie Park backpack. "That's a great idea!"

"Hold on, let me find the flame-retardant spray." Vivian digs through her bag and pulls out a spray can. She twists the cap open and holds it up to me. "Turn around and I'll spray you."

"Spray me? Why?"

"Jet packs can't turn on without a flame, and I don't want you catching on fire."

"Oh, okay. That makes sense." I turn around and Vivian sprays the back of my body. I pull up the thermal imaging goggles so that they're resting on the top of my head.

"All right," Vivian says, putting the spray can back into her backpack and zipping it up. She stands up and puts her hands on the backpack straps, looking at me. "All you need to do is say 'adventure pack, turn on the jet pack.' " As she says this, small flames erupt out of the back of her backpack. "Except, in your case, you call it a backup adventure pack."

"Okay," I say. I feel nervous. What if the flame-retardant spray doesn't work on Earth clothes? What if my jet pack goes out of control and I crash through the trees? Then I remember that my mission is to find Ruby and Hudson, and using a jet pack is probably the fastest way to do that.

I take a deep breath, grab onto the straps in the front of my backpack, and state, "Backup adventure pack, turn on the jet pack." I start to float off of the branch. "Whoa!" I feel myself hovering midair. Part of me wants to turn off the jet pack and return my feet to the safety of the branch. There's another part of me though that just wants to fly above the trees and see how fast these things can go. I smile at Vivian, and she smiles back.

"To control the jet pack, you just have to shift the weight of your body," Vivian explains. She stretches out her arm to one side and the jet pack glides her away from the branch. She stretches her other arm back and the jet pack glides her back toward the branch.

I think about my Superman comic books. I bet this is just how he does it. Well, minus the jet pack. I stretch my arm out to my side. I feel the jet pack move me away from the branch. I don't move as smoothly as Vivian did, though. In fact, the move is very shaky.

"You get better with practice," Vivian says, gliding toward me. "Now, should we go find your friends?"

"Yes!" I pull the thermal imaging goggles off of my head and put them back over my eyes. Then I have second thoughts. The world looks so different with them on, and I feel like it will be hard enough not to crash with normal vision. "Wait!" I push the thermal imaging goggles back onto the top of my head.

"What's wrong?"

"I think the person who doesn't need jet pack practice should be the one to wear the goggles that make everything look weird."

"Ah, good thinking." Vivian reaches out her hand. I pull the goggles off and give them to her. She puts them on. "Okay, let's start over here." Vivian clenches her fists and leans her body hard away from the pond. She shoots like a torpedo in that direction.

Whoa, that was fast! I mimic Vivian, clenching my fists and leaning hard toward her. The wind flies by me as I speed toward her. This must be what it feels like to be a race car driver, except I'm not wearing a seatbelt or a helmet. *Should* I be wearing a helmet? My mom would say I should, for sure. She always makes me wear one when I'm on a bike. And that's a bike *on the ground*. In the sky on a jet pack, she'd probably have me wear a helmet and knee pads and elbow pads and football pads and an every-inch-of-your body pad. I don't think they make those though so my mom would probably improvise and just strap a mattress to the front and the back of me.

As I'm wondering if Vivian has any mattresses in her adventure pack, she leans her body upward which slows her down. It's like she's standing in mid-air. I try to do the same, but I lean too far and end up upside down. I try to lean back, and I'm upright for a second before falling upside down again.

As blood starts to drain down, no doubt turning my face bright red, I look at Vivian. She laughs and glides over to me. "Grab my arm," she says. I grip it and she pulls me upright again. We float there in the sky, scanning the world below. I don't see anything that resembles a human being. Then Vivian gasps. "There's heat in the shape of a person over there!" She points to an area of the forest below where the trees aren't as thick. I don't see anything, but I know she can see better than me since she has the goggles on. I lean my body toward the area that she's pointing to and my jet pack propels me down.

"Wait up!" Vivian calls. I don't stop, though. I'm too excited to see my friends. Vivian must have made her jet pack have super speed because soon she's right next to me.

As we zoom toward the area below, a figure becomes clearer to me. It does look like a human being. He's walking through the forest. When we're closer, I can tell he's short, like a kid. Then he looks up at us. I realize I know him. He's from Earth like I am. But it isn't Ruby, and it isn't Hudson. It's someone whom I'd never expect to see here, and someone I don't want to see here.

Terror (14)

I tilt my body upward so that I stop and stand in mid-air. I'm just above the canopy of the trees. Vivian doesn't realize I've stopped and keeps going. I watch her land next to the kid. She looks up at me. "Are you coming?" she yells.

I sigh and shift my weight so that the jet pack brings me down. I realize I haven't tried landing with a jet pack yet, and I wish I'd practiced it before now. I try to land on my feet next to Vivian, but I lose my balance and end up on my butt.

"Hahaha," the kid next to Vivian laughs.

Vivian doesn't join in on the laughter. "Are you okay?" she asks. "Don't worry about it. I landed like that my first time, too. It just takes practice."

"I know you," the kid says as I stand up and brush the leaves off my pants.

"Yeah. I know you, too," I respond. Actually, I don't know his name, but I know he's the same stout kid with thick eyebrows that I'd seen kick Tony out of his seat on the bus.

"I know how you got here, too."

"Do you?" I ask.

"Yes. You stole my glove," he says, pointing at the glove on my hand.

My jaw drops in surprise. Whoa, whoa, *whoa*. The magic glove belongs to the bully? I look at the glove on my hand and realize its match is on the bully's hand.

"You stole his glove?" Vivian asks.

"Well, not really. My friends and I found it. It was lying on the ground at the park. It's not like the park has a lost and found or anything. We didn't know who it belonged to or how we could get it back to him."

Vivian pulls a leaf out of my hair, and I continue, "Plus, the wizard told me it was our's in my dream."

"You think a dream gives you permission to steal?" the bully says, crossing his arms. He chuckles.

"I had a dream I had your backpack. I guess that means you need to give it to me."

I cross my arms, too. "This wasn't just any dream. My friend Hudson had the same one."

"Coincidence," the bully responds. "You know the glove belongs to me. I have its match. And now you can give it back to me." He puts his hand out.

I know he wants me to take the glove off and put it in his hand, but then how will I get back to Olivia? Or back home to the Earth Dimension, for that matter? "I can give it to you once my friends and I are back on Earth."

"Your *friends*?" He looks around, then looks at Vivian. "I only see one friend here, unless you have some imaginary ones?"

Vivian responds, "First of all, I don't need to go back to Earth. I mean, it would be fun to visit, but that's not my home dimension. Secondly, we're here looking for two of his friends. Then we need to go back to my dimension and get his third friend and eat some delicious food. *Then,* they need to get back to Earth."

"Okay," the bully looks at me. "I'll wait for you at the park. When you get back, you can give the glove back to me." He starts to walk away.

"Hold on!" Vivian calls. The bully doesn't turn around. "Aren't you going to help us?"

"No," he says. He starts whistling as he continues to walk away.

Vivian gives me a confused look. "Did he just whistle?" she asks quietly.

"Yeah. That was strange."

Then the bully whistles again. I hear squawking in the distance. It sounds like the crow I heard earlier. The bully whistles again and the squawking gets louder. It's coming from the sky. I look up and see a flying dinosaur. I know from my dinosaur book that it's a pterodactyl. It swoops down and lands next to the bully. "Good boy, Terror," the bully says, reaching up to pat the head of the great beast.

Vivian chuckles in amazement. "You have a pet pterodactyl?" She steps toward them. "Can I pet him?"

The bully shrugs. "I guess."

Vivian walks over, holding her hand out tentatively. Terror sniffs it, then lowers his head so Vivian can pet him. "How do you have a pet pterodactyl?"

The bully's gruff tone softens. "I found his egg the first time I came here. He hatched and I was the first thing he saw. I caught insects for him to eat, and I come back here a lot to visit him."

"That's so cool. I'm Vivian, by the way."

"I'm Bryce." Bryce pats Terror on the head again. "Do you want to see something cool?"

"Sure!"

"Step back."

Vivian takes a big step backward.

"Let's go for a ride, Terror." Terror crouches down and spreads his wings. I realize how huge he is with the movement. He's like a small airplane! Bryce climbs onto Terror's back and leans down to wrap his arms around the bottom of Terror's neck. I duck down as Terror flaps his wings and takes flight. The great gusts tousle my hair.

Vivian and I watch them fly into the sky.

"This is really happening right now?" she asks with a big grin on her face. "We're watching him fly on a *pterodactyl*? Traveling to a new dimension is the *coolest*!"

"It would be cooler if we could find Ruby and Hudson," I say, kicking a rock on the ground.

The smile fades from Vivian's face and she looks over at me. "You're right. Now we have Bryce to help us with the search. Let's jet pack up to him and we can all look together."

"I don't think he's going to help us."

"Why wouldn't he?"

"He's a bully, Vivian. He kicked Ruby's little brother out of his bus seat."

"Well, it's never too late to give someone a second chance," she says. She grabs onto her backpack straps. "Adventure pack, turn on the jet pack!" She shoots into the sky.

Hmm, do I follow her? I look toward the thick forest. If Ruby and Hudson are in there, we might not see them from the sky. I walk toward the trees. "Ruby! Hudson!" I call. I walk into the forest. The tree canopy blocks a lot of the sunlight, so my eyes take a moment to adjust to the change in brightness. "Ruby! Hudson!" I call again. I keep walking and keep my eyes on the muddy ground to watch for footprints. "Ruby! Hudson!" Then I hear a yell. My heart starts to race. "Ruby, Hudson, was that one of you?" I hear the yell again and look in the direction it came from. I don't see anyone. I run to get a closer look. I follow the sound of the yell, go around a large tree trunk, and turn next to an overgrown, thorny bush that has red berries on it.

I stop when I find myself looking at a creature that looks a lot like a goat. It's white with brown horns. It's biting off a berry from the bush. When it sees me, it raises its head to the sky and yells. It sounds just like the yell I'd heard earlier. As I stare at it, I feel disappointed. I was really hoping I'd heard one of my friends.

"Hey, fella," I say, leaning down toward the goat-thing. I don't actually *think* he'll respond, but maybe this dimension has goats who understand English. "Have you seen my friends?" The goat opens his mouth wide and I realize he's different from the goats we have on Earth. His teeth are sharp, like a sharks.

What happens next feels like it happens in slow motion. The goat steps toward me, still bearing his terrifying teeth. I know I should run, but my feet are frozen. Then the goat jerks his head and looks behind me. He closes his mouth and slowly backs away from me.

I know that something behind me must have scared him. I want to turn around to see what it is, but I'm worried about what kind of scary creature would scare off the scary goat. Then I hear a snort and a growl. I don't have to turn around to know what creature is behind me.

It's the T-rex.

It's time to use your imagination and help illustrate this story! Draw Sawyer meeting the scary goat-like creature.

Vishkurs (15)

I grab onto the straps of my backpack and yell, "Backup adventure pack, turn on the jet pack!" The jet pack turns on. I raise my fist toward the leaves above me and shoot toward the tree canopy. The T-rex growls and swings his head toward me. Oh no! Oh no, oh no, OH NO! He got me! His head crashes into my legs and I shoot toward a nearby tree, hitting its trunk. Ouch. As I fall toward the ground, I hear a squawking sound. The T-rex snorts and moves his head toward the sound.

In the distance, Terror flies under the canopy of the trees. He squawks again and the T-rex runs toward him. Terror turns around, Bryce still on his back, and flies out of the forest. The T-rex roars and chases after him. I have to get away while I can. I grab the nearest branch and start to climb the tree it belongs to.

"Sawyer!"

I look up and see Vivian is standing on a branch at the top of the tree.

"We have to get out of here before he comes back! Can you climb up here?"

I nod my head. I think about instead using the jet pack, but there'd be too many branches in the way. "I think I can." I stand up and climb up to the top.

"Are you hurt?"

I brush some leaves off of my clothes and think about her question. "My back hurts a little, but I'm okay."

"Why did you run back into the forest?"

"I heard yelling, but it turned out to just be a goat with extremely sharp teeth."

Vivian looks toward the ground. "Is the goat still down there?"

"No."

"Where'd he go?"

"He ran away from the dinosaur with even sharper teeth."

"Oh, okay. When Bryce and I were flying, I put the goggles on and saw yellow and red colors in the shape of a person. Whoever it is is toward the top of a tree near the pond. We were going to check it out but came to find you first."

"Let's go check it out now," I say.

Vivian puts her hands on her backpack straps. "Adventure pack, turn on the jet pack!" She flies upward, and I follow.

As we soar above the trees, I can see Terror and Bryce flying above the clearing. The T-rex is still chasing after them, snapping his teeth and pawing at the air with his little front claws. I feel like I'd be scared if I were in that situation, but Bryce is smiling (and, actually, it looks like Terror is smiling, too).

The T-rex stops as Terror flies higher into the air. Bryce waves at us, still smiling.

When he gets close, I say, "Thanks, a lot, you guys. You probably saved my life back there."

Bryce pats Terror on the neck. "It was our pleasure. There's nothing more fun than driving Old Rex crazy, and no one does that better than Terror here."

I hear a yell. I wonder if the scary goat is nearby. Then I see her. Standing at the top of a tall tree on a thick branch is Ruby. She's waving, smiling, jumping, and clapping. I wave back.

"Sawyer!" she yells again. I lean forward hard so I can get to her quickly.

"Hi, Ruby," I say casually as I land on the branch next to her.

Ruby fires questions at me. "How did you get here? Are you using a jet pack? Who are your friends?" Then her eyes land on Bryce and her tone changes. She sounds mad. "You!" she yells. She points at him. "You're the bully who was mean to my brother!"

I didn't know it was possible for a pterodactyl to look scared, but Terror's face fills with fear as he flies slightly backward, away from Ruby. Really? He likes being chased by a T-rex, but an eight year old girl makes him scared? "He helped me!" I say to her.

Ruby looks surprised. She crosses her arms. "No. He didn't."

"Yes. He did. He distracted a T-rex who was after me."

I hear Hudson's voice. "The T-rex came after you, too?"

"Hudson?" I look down toward where his voice had come from. He's on a branch farther down the tree. There are few things that could get him to climb this high. I guess a T-rex is one of those things.

"Hey, Sawyer," he replies. "I'm so glad you found us. We didn't know how we'd get back. Is Olivia with you?"

"No. She's back in Vivian's dimension. She hurt her foot."

"Well, now that we found your friends, we can go back there," says Vivian. "A healer is probably mending her right now."

"Sounds good," I reply. "Hudson, should we climb down by you before we travel back?"

"Yes, please."

I look at Bryce. "Um, do you want to come with us?"

"Nah, that's okay. I'm going to spend some more time with Terror." He rides away without a goodbye or a wave.

Vivian, Ruby, and I climb down the tree so we're on the same branch as Hudson. Hudson and I do our special high five. "Ready?" I ask.

"Yep," they say. We put our hands on each other's shoulders.

"Magic glove, takes us back to the Adventure Dimension!"

The swirling tube takes us back to the Adventure Dimension, and we land on the ground right next to the rope ladder.

Vivian smiles at us and puts her hand on the rope ladder. She looks at Hudson. "This is where I'm from," she says proudly. She starts to climb the ladder.

"Wait!" Ruby whispers. Vivian stops, climbs down, and stands by me. "Is Olivia up there?" Ruby asks.

"Yes," Vivian whispers back.

"We can't tell her about the T-rex."

"Why not?" Vivian asks. I think I know why, though. If Olivia hears something as dangerous as a T-rex is in another dimension, she'll never want to dimension travel again.

Hudson must be thinking the same thing we are. "Do you think it will scare her?" he asks.

"Yes. I like traveling to different dimensions, and I don't want her stopping us," Ruby replies. "Let's only tell her about Terror and Bryce and some of the good stuff."

"I don't want to lie to her," I say. "Olivia is a great friend. We should be honest with her."

"We don't have to lie. She's not going to *ask us* if there was a T-rex there. We just don't mention it." Ruby looks each of us in the eye. "Promise me none of you will tell her about the T-rex."

"Okay," Hudson and I say.

Vivian shrugs. "Okay. That's fine by me." She climbs up the rope ladder. I follow, then Ruby and Hudson.

"You found them!" Olivia exclaims when we step onto the treehouse floor. She's sitting at a table with a fork in her hand and a plate in front of her. Victor is sitting in a chair next to her.

"How's your foot?" I ask.

"All better. The healer fixed it in minutes." She gives me a thumb's up.

"We ordered food. Are you guys hungry?" Victor asks.

"Starving," Vivian replies. She sits in a chair next to Victor. She looks at the food on Olivia's plate. "What do you think of vishkurs?"

"It's so delicious! I can't stop eating it."

"It is really good," says Victor. "Come on, Sawyer and friends, come try some."

We all sit down at the table. "Wait, where did this table and chairs come from, anyway?" I ask. These weren't here when I left.

"The food delivery girl brought it." Victor scoops some of the food from the container and puts it on each of our plates. It looks like a pasta dish with toppings on it like you'd see on a pizza, but the toppings don't look like any toppings we have on Earth.

"Oh." I take a bite of the vishkurs. Yum! It's so good. It tastes like the most delicious pizza I've ever had.

Vivian takes a bite of her vishkurs, and then she looks at Victor and Olivia. "I'm really glad we brought the adventure pack with us. It came in handy when we were trying to find Ruby and Hudson."

"What was the dimension that you guys were in like?" Olivia asks.

Ruby responds, "There were lots of trees that were really fun to climb. And there were pterodactyls!"

"Pterodactyls? Was that scary?"

"Not at all."

"And you'll never guess who else was there," Hudson adds.

"Who?"

"Remember that bully who kicked Tony out of his seat on the bus?"

Olivia's jaw drops. "What?" She shakes her head in disbelief. "The bully was in that dimension?"

I wonder if I should stick up for Bryce. He did save me from the T-rex, after all. But then I'd probably have to bring up the T-rex, and I promised Ruby I wouldn't. "Yes, and he has a pet pterodactyl named Terror, and he rides on him."

Olivia still looks surprised. "Was he nice to you guys there?"

"Pretty nice," I say. "Well, except he told me I have to give him his glove back."

"*His* glove?" Hudson asks.

I nod. "Yeah. This magic glove is his. He has the one for the other hand."

Hudson looks disappointed. "Oh."

Ruby reaches her hand toward me. "Give me the glove, Sawyer."

I wonder why she wants it. Is she ready for us to go back to Earth? I take the glove off and hand it to her.

She puts it on and then crosses her arms. "We're not giving this back to him."

"Ruby! It's his property!" Olivia says.

"Is it really? How do we know he didn't just find it like we found ours? Besides, the bus seat was Tony's property, and Bryce stole that from him. It's time the bully got a taste of his own medicine."

Ruby has a point. Bryce wasn't nice to sweet, little Tony. Why should we be nice to Bryce? Then I remember again that Bryce and Terror saved me from a huge, carnivorous dinosaur and I feel guilty. "No, Ruby, we need to give it back to Bryce."

Victor clears his throat. "Why don't you guys take a vote? Who thinks you all should keep the glove?"

Ruby's hand shoots up.

Hudson puts his hand up, too. "He only needs one of the gloves to dimension travel. I think we should buy him another cotton glove from the store that is the same color as this one, but we keep the other magic one."

That's also a good point.

Victor raises his hand, too. "I'm not sure if I count, but I think you should keep the glove, too. I like you guys and I want you to visit us again." He looks at Olivia, then me. Neither of us has raised our hand.

"Does that mean both of you think you should give the glove back to Bryce?"

"Yes," we say together.

"I do, too," Vivian says. "Bryce seemed pretty cool to me."

"I guess we have a tie," Olivia says. She scrapes her almost-empty plate with her fork and puts it in her mouth. The rest of us finish eating as well. "We need to get back to Earth now." She looks at Victor and Vivian. "It was great meeting you! Thank you for the food, and for having the healer fix my foot."

Vivian smiles at Olivia and gives her a hug. "You're welcome! I hope I see you guys again soon." She then gives each of the rest of us a hug.

We put our hands on one another's shoulders. Ruby says, "Magic glove, take us back to the Earth Dimension."

As we fly through the swirling tube, I think about how Bryce will probably be waiting for us at the park when we get there. He's going to demand Ruby give him the glove. Knowing Ruby, she'll refuse to give it to him. I wonder what will happen from there. Will Bryce tell his parents? Will he tell Ruby's parents? I feel sad because I know we need to give it back, but dimension travel is so much fun.

Our feet touch the ground and I look around for Bryce. The park is deserted. Everyone else looks around, too.

Olivia takes the X3 watch off and hands it to me. "Thanks for letting me borrow this."

"You're welcome." I take it back and put it on my wrist. I feel something hit my back.

Ruby gasps. "The pine cone thrower!" She runs toward the rock climbing wall. We follow, but Ruby is fast. Before the rest of us get there, she gets to the other side of it. She puts her hands on her hips, and yells, "You!"

I reach the wall and see Bryce is behind it. He looks at me, laughs, and throws another pine cone at me. It hits me in the chest. "Got you again!" he says.

I do *not* like this kid. I like him even less when he says, "Alright. Give me my glove back now." He reaches his hand out to Ruby.

Ruby crosses her arms. "No. We decided we're not giving it back to you."

Hudson holds up his hand. "Look, we had an idea. You only need one glove to dimension travel, so how about we keep this one, but we buy you a glove that's the same color for your other hand?"

Bryce keeps his hand reached out toward Ruby. "That doesn't work for me. Give me back my glove."

"We found it, fair and square," Ruby says.

"It's *mine*, fair and square."

"Where did you get it, anyway?" Olivia asks.

"That's none of your business," Bryce replies stubbornly, crossing his arms.

"You stole it from someone, didn't you?" Ruby asks.

"No."

"Then how did you get it?"

"My uncle gave it to me."

"Oh really? And how did your uncle get it?"

"He made it after he helped discover dimension travel."

"Oh, yeah? Who did he discover that with?"

"You're stalling. Just give the glove to me. I want to go home and play video games."

I realize Ruby probably is stalling. What's the point? I feel sad, but I know, even if we don't do it now, we'll probably give his glove back to him eventually. "Just give him the glove, Ruby."

Olivia chimes in with equal sadness in her tone. "Yeah, just give him the glove."

Ruby looks at Hudson, probably thinking he'll disagree. He doesn't. "Argh," she scoffs. "Fine!" She takes the glove off and throws it at Bryce.

Bryce catches it and walks away without saying anything else. He walks into the house that's right next to Zombie Park, the one that had been for sale.

Ruby groans. "Aw, man, he lives right next to our park! That stinks!"

I nod. The crew and I come here basically every day and I don't want Bryce bothering us. I sigh sadly and kick a rock on the ground. I look at Olivia. "Want to head home together?"

She nods. I do my special handshakes with Hudson and Ruby. Olivia and I grab our scooters and slowly ride toward our houses.

"I know we did the right thing," Olivia says, sadness in her voice. "But I'm going to miss dimension travel."

"Yeah. It would have been cool to go visit Alex and Vivian and everyone again."

"Right." We don't talk for the rest of the way to Olivia's house. She waves goodbye to me and I keep going to my house.

As I'm going up the driveway, I hear someone whisper loudly, "Pssst, Sawyer!" I stop and look toward the voice. A boy steps out from between some ever-green trees. I recognize who he is as soon as I notice his spiky yellow hair.

X4 **16**

"Alex!" I say with a smile. "You look different." Although he still has spiky yellow hair, his skin is no longer purple. It's peach, like mine.

Alex smiles back. "Yeah. The tunnel changed my skin color when I was going through it. I'm sure it will go back to purple when I'm back in the Sports Dimension."

"What are you doing here? How did you find me? And do you still have the football pox?"

"No. Dad and his team invented a medicine that gets rid of it. I'm here to see you. I found you because the watch you're wearing sends out a GPS signal that I tracked. I have something for you!" Alex takes his backpack off and digs through it. He pulls out a box and hands it to me.

I open it. Inside is a watch that looks a lot like my X3 watch. It has a gray band and a digital screen with the time showing on it.

"It's an upgraded watch! Dad calls it the X4. It can do everything the X3 watch does, but it can also do more."

"Awesome! Thank you! What more can it do?"

"Well, you won't need the magic glove anymore."

"We won't? Why not?"

His response makes my smile widen. "Because the X4 watch will let you dimension travel."

Now make up your own dimension! Draw it here.

Are you still flipping pages? The book is over. Go play outside.

Seriously, go play outside. Get some fresh air. Throw a ball.

The End

For real, this is the end. Of the book. Not the world.
Thanks for reading!

Made in the USA
Monee, IL
02 June 2021